TIME TRAVELERS BOOK # 1

DEMONS *of* TIME

RACE TO THE SEVENTH SUNSET

VARUN SAYAL

ISBN : 978-93-5351-893-6

ABOUT THE AUTHOR

Varun Sayal is a science fiction author who has built considerable repute in the writing world within a short span of time. His début work 'Time Crawlers' has been a phenomenal hit on Amazon. It has also been very well received by the Goodreads Reader community. Testimony to that fact is over three hundred positive reviews on GoodReads, Amazon and other platforms, within just six months of publishing that book.

DEDICATED TO MY PARENTS;
I AM WHAT I AM TODAY,
BECAUSE OF THEM.
AND TO MY LOVELY WIFE,
WHO IS THE SOURCE
OF ALL MY STRENGTH
AND HAPPINESS.

TABLE OF CONTENTS

1

KUMBH AND VETRI, THE TIME-DEMONS

Dandak Forest, India | Year 3077 BC

An eight-year-old boy and a woman in her early thirties sprinted across the jungle. Feeble moonlight illuminated their path. The two shadows chasing them drew closer. The child scampered in his short pants, but the woman's long-robed *saree* was slowing her down. As they ran for their lives through the jungle, the thorny bushes tore at their clothes and scratched their skin. Their feet bled from the sharp stones and twigs on their way. Out of breath, gasping for air, they dashed through the forest for their lives.

"How far, Mother?" the child asked.

The mother pushed the son, ensuring he kept his pace. "Right behind that line of trees, son. Don't slow down."

The son stumbled over a sharp-edged stone and slipped. His mother halted to come back and help him up. She froze in terror as she realized the two shadows had finally caught up with them. They now stood only a few feet away from her, glaring at her and the child.

"Please don't kill my son. I'm the one who planned this escape. Please let him go," Mother implored, her hands folded in a plea.

One shadow came forward, out of the shade. His ravenous face and athletic body looked menacing in the murky light of the overcast night. His well-built, brawny torso was drenched with sweat, and he was wheezing because of the chase. His hair was long and stringy, hanging around enormous eyes. With rugged dark green trousers below, he was naked from the waist up. A long necklace made of human and goat skulls was hanging around his neck. In his right hand, he clutched a huge, shining metal hammer stained with old, dried blood.

He was *Kumbh*, also known as *Kaal-daitya*, a demon of time. Kumbh came closer to the mother and the son, sat down on his knees, and looked right into the mother's eyes.

He spoke in a sardonic tone. "This is your third crack at running away in last two months, right? I assumed you were more likely to fight than flee. Your belligerent personality made you so appealing. In fact, I loved the fact that I hated this fight in you. Or I hated the fact that I loved it. Either way, I think this stupid son of yours is the reason you're losing your best qualities. He'll have to pay the price for your treacherous attempt to escape. I warned you the last time. Did I not?"

His giant face further widened with a sinister smile that floated on his filthy scarred lips. His wide, blood-stained incisors clenched together.

The second shadow also walked out of the shades. He was *Vetri*, the twin brother of Kumbh, another time-demon. He wore a similar attire and he had a long strand of barbed wire in his hands, which he was twisting and pulling as if readying himself to strangle a human being.

"Brother, why don't we kill this child and feed him to the wild animals? After that, we'll tie this wretched woman by her legs using this rope, and drag her all the way back to our palace. This is the best way to teach her the right lesson," Vetri said. He licked the barbed wire with his coarse, blackened tongue.

Mother pleaded again, "No, no, please don't kill my boy! I'll do whatever you want; take my life instead. I committed this mistake, not him."

"We can't kill you, can we? We need you, Dhara. We need you in our bed to brighten our lonely nights." Vetri let out a burst of laughter. "Brother, I have an idea. Why don't we let these two run a few more miles in the jungle while we chase them? I was enjoying this whole chase, this hunt. It reminded me of the times when we used to make lowly village kids run through the forest while we chased them, and then impaled their skulls on our javelins."

Kumbh cut off Vetri. "Enough. We need to end this now. You take the bitch back to the night palace. I will finish off this kid and scatter his bone shards around the jungle. It's been a long time since I enjoyed a good cattle-smashing." He smelled his hammer as if relishing the stench emanating from it.

"Why do you always snub me, brother?" Vetri retorted. Pitch-drunk, he wasn't in a mood to take orders, especially in front of their slaves.

"I didn't mean to," Kumbh pacified him. "But we don't have time for a playful chase. In the heat of the moment, we came running after this woman. Our bodyguards and imperial protection army, none of them are here. We need to finish them and head back right away."

There was a sudden movement in the bushes nearby, and both Kumbh and Vetri stiffened. Dhara and the child also stood up and gaped at the bushes.

From within the woods emerged an old hermit. He was the renowned sage Guru *Rigu*. His long white hair was tied on top of his head. His thick white mustache and a big beard covered most of his wrinkled face. He had a long dark red cloth tied around his waist, and he wore a few sacred bead-necklaces around his frail, attenuated torso. In his left hand, he clutched a metal pot, and a bright creamy-white color conch-shell in his right hand.

Rigu spoke in a soft tone. "Kumbh and Vetri, you are standing within the confines of the holy *Dandak* forest. This forest has not seen a sin committed on its soil since the last thousand years. Why don't you two leave this poor woman and her child alone? In return, I promise I will allow you two to leave this place, with no harm."

Kumbh smirked and clamped on his hammer with indignation. He pointed his finger at Rigu. "You? You promise that you will allow us to leave this place without any harm? How kind of you, old man. But since you already know our names, you must also know who we are. You must know that even the most powerful sages and their curse-laden holy waters cannot scratch us. So why don't you take your puny threats and go continue your night-stroll in peace? If you stay, this may be your last night alive."

Rigu smiled. "I know very well who you are. You both lived as the ancient demons Trikaati and Vapaati a few centuries ago when you slaughtered and cannibalized your enemy tribes. Two hundred years ago, you wreaked havoc as the bloodthirsty princes Trilesh and Vapt, when you mercilessly incinerated ten thousand large villages and their inhabitants. Men, women, children, and cattle were annihilated. For what? So that you could win a bet over who could destroy more lives in one day.

"Then you also went a few thousand years in the future and became the barbaric Mongol invaders Temüjin and his twin brother Vladüjin. There, you waged wars, took millions of innocent lives, and caused decades of endless bloodshed in name of conquering the land. The list of your heinous crimes is endless. You can crawl through time and land your consciousnesses into whichever innocent bodies you like; possess them, control them, and cause endless death and misery wherever you go. You have no ethical accountability—and that is not acceptable. Time travel is a power, a blessing, a gift, which you could have used to serve humanity. Instead, you have abused it to take countless lives over the centuries."

Rigu's words stunned Kumbh and Vetri, and they stood unmoved. There was silence in the forest for a few moments.

Then Kumbh spoke. "I reckon that you're a time-reader. Normal human beings don't know those things about us. I loathe your kind because, like a silent serpent, you read and document our movements and secrets. I believed we wiped out your race around five hundred years ago. I strangled the last known time-reader sage Alek with these very hands. But it seems we were wrong in assuming you all were gone for good."

Rigu felt an angry expression grow on his face. He controlled himself.

Kumbh was more alert and careful too. He knew that time-readers could selectively read the past, present, and future. Armed with this knowledge, time-readers were their only truly formidable enemies. He realized Rigu would not have walked into this situation without doing a time-reading of it. The sage would have weighed a lot of permutations and combinations of what was about to go down.

Kumbh took a quick look at his surroundings as he addressed Rigu. "You knew what kind of beasts we are. Yet you believe that you can somehow defeat us today and get out of here alive? You knew that we would come here, right at this moment. Why did you walk into the arms of death like this? There are far easier ways to commit suicide, old man. You don't have a lot of days left in your dismal life, given your old age and your already gangly body."

Vetri cut him short and grabbed Dhara's arm. "Why are you talking so much? Let's kill this old sage and the kid, and let's go home. I'm yearning for another drink, and this is annoying." Vetri was not much of a thinker, because his brother did most of the planning for both of them.

As Vetri was about to drag Dhara along with him, he felt a sudden sharp pain on his wrist. He had to let go of the woman. Her boy has dug his teeth sharply into his wrist and was not letting go.

"You little snake! I'll slaughter you!" Vetri slapped the boy, who fell on the ground, unconscious. As Vetri bent to grab the boy by his neck and strangle him, Rigu quickly splashed the water from his metal pot on both Vetri and Kumbh.

Both of them froze for a moment, anticipating some kind of curse to administer or some sort of chemical reaction to occur. But nothing happened. Both of them looked at each other and cachinnated.

"This was your holy water, old fool? See? It had no impact on us." Vetri chuckled. "I told you, we're unassailable. Was this even holy water, or were you carrying that for your late night ablutions?" Both of them sneered and mocked Rigu.

Rigu lowered his head. "My holy water didn't work. I was sure it would, but it didn't. You are formidable entities indeed. I admit I underestimated your divinity. I know you'll kill me, but the person who is about to die is usually granted one last wish. You two are benevolent emperors, rulers of this universe. I hope you will grant me one last wish—a dying man's last desire?"

"I want to take my hammer and crush your skull right now," Kumbh cautioned. He raised his hammer to Rigu's forehead and touched it as if taking aim. "You won't even feel a thing, old man. But your last wish intrigues me. Go on, tell me, what do you want to do before I swing my hammer? And yes, don't try any tricks. I won't take more than a moment to drop you."

Rigu took a deep breath and looked at the conch-shell in his hand. "I wanted to blow my sacred conch-shell, my *shakti-shankha*, one last time. This holy conch-shell has been passed on as a family legacy from my grandfather to my father, and then to me. Our ancestors believed if we blew this conch-shell right before our death, it's sound-waves will take us to heaven after our demise," Rigu pleaded.

Vetri chuckled. "Go on. We grant your last wish. I will count to five, and after that, Kumbh will smash your head."

"No! Don't move an inch, time-reader!" Kumbh thundered. "Vetri, we don't know what this sage will do with this conch-shell. He's a time-reader, and you know these treacherous bastards. They seldom confront us without razor-sharp preparations. With this conch-shell, he may be calling for help. An army may be moving in our direction as we speak. Let's get out of here." Kumbh put his hand on Vetri's shoulder and pressed it lightly.

"Hold on, do you think I'm stupid?" Vetri pushed Kumbh away, his eyes drowsy with drunken torpor.

"No, I don't think you're stupid."

"No—what do you mean? By allowing him to blow some puny conch-shell, I'm threatening our safety? Because I'm an imbecile?"

"Did I say that?"

"No, but you meant that. You constantly question my decisions, don't you? We are time-demons, my brother! This stupid old man can do us no harm. Don't you understand?"

"I do, but…"

"But what? What? We are the kings of the world. When people are dying in front of us, we grant them last wishes. That is our culture. Our legacy."

Kumbh gave up. It was another irritable mood that made Vetri completely lose the sense of what was in their best interests. At such times, he only viewed the world through the lens of his fragile ego.

"All right, geezer. Go ahead."

"No! I'll give this order." Vetri protested again.

"Yes sir, will you please give this order?" Kumbh said and bowed a little.

Vetri grinned like a dunce. He loved these small victories over his brainy brother. He addressed Rigu. "Hey, you time-reading insect! Go ahead, blow your conch-shell. But this better not be another vacuous trick of yours. Otherwise, we'll torture you for days before we take your life. Go on. I, Lord Vetri, permit you to fulfill your dying wish."

Rigu instantly threw the metal pot to the side, then clenched the conch-shell with both his hands. He pressed it to his lips and blew with the full force of his throat. A deep trumpeting blast resonated through the forest. It went higher and higher in pitch, finally fading to a complete close. The waves of sound kept echoing for a few moments throughout the desolated vicinity.

Kumbh picked up his hammer and touched its blunt claw to Rigu's head as if taking aim. He lifted the hammer and was about to strike Rigu when his hands and arms stiffened.

"Now, get ready to die, son of a …why can't I move? I can't move, Vetri! What's happening? Are you able to move? What's this monkey magic, sage? What have you done?" Kumbh thundered in anger. He struggled to move his arms, but he was completely frozen. He couldn't move a single muscle.

"I can't move either…my neck is stiff. I cannot…" Vetri attempted to speak, but his throat, his mouth, and his tongue felt so dry as if they were made of stone.

Rigu had a victorious smile on his face. His trick had worked. "Chemical-induced paralytic shock, catalyzed by sound waves—an anesthetic potion I have been working on for some time. Well, since the moment I saw the vision, I knew you both would come to Dandak Forest today. The innocent holy water I splashed on you was actually that anesthetic.

"While we engaged in conversation, this chemical entered your body through your skin and spread through your system. When I blew the conch-shell, the sonic waves catalyzed the paralytic properties of the chemical. You are both completely immobilized. You can't move, you can't speak. You couldn't even tilt your eyeballs if you wanted to. The effect of this incapacitating dosage will stay on for a few hours. In a few moments, you will feel delirious as the chemicals reach your brain and put you into a deep sleep."

Both Kumbh and Vetri shook their heads as if overcome with a fit. They then collapsed on the ground and lay there, unconscious.

Dhara picked up her son and tightly hugged him, sobbing. He was still unconscious. Rigu approached them and put his hand on her head. She looked at Rigu with gratitude in her eyes. She couldn't believe that Rigu had subdued such powerful devils. He had saved her and her son from imminent torture and death.

"What will happen now? What will happen to me and my son?" she asked.

With a satisfied smile, Rigu sat on a grass patch nearby. "Your son is a brave kid. He fought for you, even used his teeth as a weapon when he felt your life was in danger. He'll be fine. He was only knocked unconscious by Vetri's blow. I have medicine at my ashram which will heal both of you in no time."

"Nothing can heal me, *Gurudev*," Dhara addressed the guru by his proper title, "Gurudev." "These animals have beaten, raped, and ravaged me for the past several years—both myself and many other women like me. Seeing those atrocities over the years, I've lost a sense of purpose. My soul feels shattered. I would have taken my life long ago, but I am only alive because of my son. I don't want any healing, Gurudev, I only want to take care of him." Dhara burst into tears.

Controlling herself she spoke again, with determination. "Now I want to get away from this land. Somewhere far, where no one can hurt me and my son. I have escaped many times, but they always caught me, as they did today. For now, they are insensate, as you say, but when they wake up, they will come for me again. I am scared, Gurudev. Please help me."

Rigu consoled her. "You don't have to worry anymore. They aren't going anywhere."

"But no jail can hold them. You know better than me that these time-demons are not tied to their flesh. They can uproot their consciousness out of a body, ride the waves of time, and enter another body at another time. How can anyone in this universe subjugate them? And how could God create such evil beings and impart such powers to them? Is there even a benevolent God who cares for us?"

"Kid, they may be the masters of time, but they are not above the Goddess of time, *Trikaaldevi*. She exists in all time-slices and watches over everything. Since Kumbh and Vetri can manipulate time, I will put them in a place where there is no concept of time—a *Kaalshoonya*, a zilch-space devoid of time as a dimension. They won't be able to escape anywhere from that prison. Don't worry. My disciples will be here shortly. They'll bind these demons in heavy-duty metal chains and take them to my science-sanctum. I've already planned to send them to that prison. Let's leave this place. My ashram is nearby. Sisters there have good medical training. They will take care of you and your son."

Dhara finally wore a bleak smile on her face. For a moment, she wanted to believe that everything would be all right. Deep in her heart, she was skeptical—there was no way this was all over. She wiped her tears, touched the feet of Rigu to take his blessings.

"I am sorry, Gurudev, I didn't even introduce myself. My name is *Dhara*. And my son's name is …"

"I know. His name is *Tejaswi*. And you call him *Tej*."

2
UNIVERSITY OF TIME-READERS

Rigu's Ashram | Few Hours Later

Rigu, his twenty disciples, and sixty security guards entered his ashram, carrying the giant bodies of Kumbh and Vetri. It was akin to a grand procession, both eerie and prodigious. Ten fortified guards walked in the front, with large fiery torches held high, leading the way; dawn was a few hours off, and the night was at its peak darkness.

Following them was Rigu on foot, with a prayer on his lips and his head held high. He had a necklace of black beads, on which he kept the count of his incantation. Alongside Rigu was a small palanquin with four sturdy bearers carrying Dhara and Tej. Behind them were Kumbh and Vetri, each carried on a huge wooden cart, one after the other, their bodies tied in thick iron chains. Ten muscular men pulled each cart, while twenty armed guards accosted them. Ten armed men walked at the end of the convoy in an attack stance.

Rigu had strong relations with several neighboring kingdoms. The cutting-edge research happening in the ashram was shared with the kings regularly. In return, those monarchs invested in the ashram's upkeep and security. They provided financial help and hired soldiers for the safekeeping of the establishment. Those were the troops Rigu was using for the safety of this convoy.

Over five hundred inhabitants of the ashram gathered around the gates. Students, medical staff, cooks, gardeners and security personnel; all were there to witness the spectacle. They looked on in awe as the parade entered the ashram. It was no small event, after all—those were two of the most nefarious time-demons.

These lethal legends had carved tales of blood, gore and senseless violence on the slates of time throughout the ages. The specters who had haunted the world of humans for millennia had finally been apprehended. The herculean task Rigu had been planning for fifteen years was over.

As soon as Rigu entered the ashram premises, he scattered the crowd. He didn't want to make a large display out of this capture. Then he started assigning duties to the staff.

Rigu sent Kumbh and Vetri to a fortified shack, which was to be under heavy guard at all times. He knew if they woke up, they would escape from those mortal bodies within seconds—although he had other plans for them. He sent Dhara and Tej to the medical center, where the staff would attend to their wounds.

Rigu himself headed to the most secluded part of the ashram. It was called the research center for hazardous chemicals.

Twenty security personnel saluted and gave way

for Rigu to enter via a large door into the center. But "hazardous chemicals" was a front, to divert attention away from the isolated premises. It was actually a secret center of excellence established by Rigu fifteen years ago. The place housed over three hundred special disciples, gifted men and women with the power to read time. These individuals were called Time-Readers.

Two years ago, Rigu had divided the whole center into three groups. He named them *Vart*, the present, *Bhavi*, the future and *Kara*, the prison. Each group comprised a hundred time-readers, seven sketch artists, three scribes, and one group leader. Sketch artists sat with the time-readers and helped capture the time-visions through vivid sketches. Scribes documented the visions and organized them using a multi-layered archiving system.

Rigu met the team leaders of each of the groups. He liked to address them by their designations, *Vart-pati*, *Bhavi-pati*, and *Kara-pati*.

"Vart-pati, I am delighted with your results." Rigu placed his hand on Vart-pati's head as he bowed to touch the guru's feet. "We've found and captured Kumbh and Vetri at their weakest point. They were alone, without their security, outside their territory. And the best part is that they were drunk. Their judgment was shaky, and their instincts were weak. Exactly as I wanted them. You actually served them to me on a plate." Rigu smiled.

Vart-pati was overjoyed but remained humble in his demeanor. "The team and I are ecstatic over our victory, and are ready for any further services."

"Ah. Victory is still out of our grasp." Rigu grimaced.

"For which I will look forward to Kara-pati. What do we have? I need a stable time-prison, and I need it now. The paralytic chemical will keep them asleep at most till sunrise. After which they'll wake up, leave their bodies, and be gone forever."

Kara-pati gulped. "We have a viable contender for a time-prison, Gurudev, but …"

"But?"

"If you can come with me to our chamber, I can explain to you a few options we have and the most pressing choice."

"All right. I'll spend the next few hours with the Kara group, as time is of the essence. I'll meet both of you later."

"Before you go, Gurudev, there was an accident." Bhavi-pati fumbled for words.

"Accident? How?"

"Two of the time-readers, they were following Kumbh's path to the future. They saw him entering the supermassive black hole." Bhavi-pati wiped the sweat off his forehead.

"Let me guess, they decided to peek inside?"

"Yes, Gurudev."

Rigu clenched his eyes and grimaced in pain. He had given all time-readers in the university a stringent mandate. They were not allowed to direct their time-reading visions beyond the event horizon of a black hole. Rigu had cast this rule in stone. He knew that black holes not only captured light but also engulfed time through invisible dimensions. Thus, a time-reader looking inside a black hole would lose himself in its endless mazes.

Only time-demons could use black holes as time-portals. Yet, once in a while, adventurous time-readers committed the cardinal mistake. Their sheer curiosity led to their cognitive demise.

"As a leader of Bhavi group you are supposed to set up best practices of time-visioning the future. Why this slip?" Rigu was stern.

Bhavi-Pati avoided Rigu's gaze.

Rigu wanted to chastise Bhavi-Pati more. But he knew this was not the best time. "How are they doing now?"

"They have both lost their senses, Gurudev. Right after their time-reading, they got aggressive. They defecated in public, tore off their clothes, and even attacked a few other disciples. We have kept them under tranquilizers, bound in chains."

"All right Bhavi-Pati. We will house them in our center for mental health for the rest of their lives. Also, inform their dependents. The ashram will take care of their families until they have another breadwinner."

"Will that involve a lot of money, Gurudev?"

"You let me take care of the finances, Bhavi-pati. I will be meeting several kings over the course of the next few months. In the past, many have shown an interest in funding the extensive research we undertake here. Now, let me speak with Kara-pati about a critical issue at our hands."

Rigu sent other two team leads away and walked over to the Kara chamber.

The main office of the Kara chamber was a small room. It had a few chairs and a table on which several sketches and documents were spread out. The Kara group had the most daunting task of all: to find a time-prison. A time prison was a place, a realm or even a virtual reality where time was non-existent, or immaterial.

Rigu knew that a time-prison was the only place where the time-demons could be incarcerated. There were places where time was absent, but finding these places was like looking for an atomic needle in a cosmic haystack. The outcome of this group was the most critical and Rigu was most worried about it.

"So, what do you have for me, Kara-pati?" Rigu smiled. "Into which timeless space of the past do you want to throw Kumbh and Vetri?" He could sense the positive nervousness in Kara-pati. He was going to unravel the results of his past two years' hard work.

"Not the past, Gurudev, the future. We have located a time-prison in the future," Kara-pati blabbered. He handed some documents over to Rigu, who started flipping through them.

The documents impressed Rigu, but he showed no emotion. Finding a time prison was no mean task. Finding one in the future was even more remarkable. The future, being the sum product of trillions of choices taken by billions of individuals, was forever tumultuous and flickering. The solution proposed in those documents was a bit far-fetched, but not impossible.

"This is good, Kara-pati."

"Do you think it will work, Gurudev?"

"I don't doubt it will work. But unlike the time-prisons which we've encountered in the past, will it hold the fort for eternity? I don't think so."

"What should we do, then?"

"Let's go ahead with the incarceration. We have no choice."

"Will you be there, Gurudev?"

"Of course I will be there. What kind of question is that? Let's start the preparations."

"I will get on it right away." Kara-pati bowed and rushed out of the room.

Rigu closed his eyes and went into deep contemplation. His fifteen years of hard work were finally culminating, yet victory looked more distant now than ever. There are times when after conquering one significant milestone in the journey, we realize the benign ignorance we had about the colossal challenges posed by the next milestone. The work was not yet done. Rigu got up and walked towards the Bhavi group's chamber.

Bhavi-pati welcomed Rigu in his office. Bhavi group's single focus was to conduct periodic readings of a specific apocalyptic event from the distant future. Kumbh and Vetri were a part—rather, the cause—of this apocalyptic event. After their recent capture, Rigu was eager to know if group Bhavi was witnessing a change in the outcome of this future event.

"Hope you've tied together the time-visions of the apocalypse from all your time readers. If so, I'd like to review them."

"Yes, Gurudev."

"And do you see a change in the visions?"

"There are many futures happening, Gurudev, so there are changes."

"What did I tell you, Bhavi-pati? I don't care about the many futures. I only care for the dominant future, the vision which is being seen by most of your time-readers."

"Yes. There is a slight change in the dominant future, Gurudev. Vetri is no longer seen in the visions. It's only Kumbh."

"That's strange—they're always together. Anyhow, the future is what it is. We can only hope to change it. Tell me. Today, we are going to imprison both of them. Do you feel there would be a change in the visions after that?"

"I am not sure, Gurudev."

"All right. Get the people together. Each time-reader, scribe, and sketch artist should receive the message. We will narrate the apocalypse to everyone."

"But why, Gurudev?"

"The disciples of the time-readers university have worked hard for this future-altering mission. They have put countless hours over the past few years and slogged until this very moment. In a few hours, we will work towards imprisoning Kumbh and Vetri forever. I don't know how that will turn out. It might have the gravest of consequences. The pupils in this center have a right to know what we've worked for, and what impact it may have on the future."

Bhavi-pati's ecstatic smile shifted to dour nervousness. He had assumed that the guru would listen to his final version of the future and pat him on the back for work well done. But now the Rigu would display his years of toil out in the open, in front of the whole university. He had not prepared for this kind of scrutiny.

"Is there a problem, Bhavi-pati?"

"No, Gurudev."

"Go ahead, gather them. They should be ready to hear a message from the future."

3
TRISILLEX, THE DEVIL FROM 2072 AD

few minutes later, a crowd of disciples gathered in the university's large central hall. They faced a dais where Guru Rigu and three group leaders were to be seated. Folks in the crowd chit-chatted, joking, speculating on why they were gathered there. Barring a few rare visits to the outer world, they were not allowed to leave the time-reader university. But the word of Kumbh and Vetri's capture had spread like wildfire. Each of them was eager to hear more from Rigu.

The crowd bustled and murmured until Rigu and the three group leads entered the room. The noise went down a few notches, but some folks continued their conversations.

Rigu stood on the dais with a smile on his face, waiting for the crowd to placate, and didn't say a word. He kept observing the crowd, taking in their youthful energy. A few in the crowd noticed that Rigu had arrived on the stage, and they started shushing each other. Within a few seconds, there was silence in the whole chamber, enough to hear a pin drop.

At last, Rigu spoke. "For a long time, I didn't know who my enemy was. By my enemy, I mean the enemy of all of humankind. I was a strong, capable time-reader, like you young souls. I could see the blood, the gore, the violence we humans inflict upon each other in the past, present, and future. I used to wonder why it happens.

"Eventually, I realized the existence of some evil, power-hungry entities who were behind most of the carnage in the world. These entities are what we call time-demons. These parasites have immense powers. Their immortality and ability to travel through time render them invincible.

"As I came in touch with more seasoned time-readers, I learned more about these devils and their atrocities against humankind. That is when I pledged to capture two of the most notorious time-demons. Today, I am too old to read time visions with clarity. Age has corroded my abilities. But I am fortunate enough to have each of you with me. To fight alongside me in this righteous quest."

Rigu took a pause and looked at the crowd. Their inquisitive faces fixed on his own.

"Now, you must be wondering why I called you to this chamber in the middle of the night. My children, I have great news. I'm sure some of you have heard it by now. But it's my duty to apprise you that after years of meticulous planning, and through efforts by some of you, Kumbh and Vetri have been finally captured."

"Yay!" one of the disciples in the crowd screamed. The whole horde broke into loud jeers of victory and started cheering. Rigu raised his hands and signaled the crowd to calm down. It was a full minute before the mob of young men and women fell silent.

"As I speak, Kara-pati is making arrangements for us to put these time-demons into a deep, dark pit—a prison from which they, hopefully, cannot escape again. Their absence from this world would be our best gift to mankind, to the generations of the future. But today, I want to reveal to you why I, fifteen years ago, embarked on this mission of capturing Kumbh and Vetri. Why was it so critical to capture them?"

The crowd was more anxious now. One-third of them were from the Bhavi group, and they knew exactly what Guru was going to say. They had been concentrating on the events of the future for the past two years. The others were eager to know.

"I tasked the Bhavi group with the reading of four years of time in the future, from the year 2069 to 2073 AD, which interest us. After Kumbh and Vetri's capture, I asked them to do a complete read of these four years once again. The idea behind this re-read was to see if we were able to change the outcome."

Rigu made eye contact with Bhavi-pati, who nodded in affirmation.

"One of the time-readers from the Bhavi group will narrate this vision of an apocalyptic future. Being time-readers, you know that in the distant future, we would be a scientifically advanced civilization. The terminology—the names, places, and technologies which you hear about during this narration—should not be a shock to you. After hearing this, if you have questions, please reach out to your respective group leaders. You may also talk to me later. Through this narration, I want you to understand the gravity of the righteous cause we are fighting for. I want you to assimilate the damning consequences of the apocalypse we are fighting to avert."

Rigu signaled Bhavi-pati to begin. He asked one of the time-readers, Kuntala, to step onto the stage. Kuntala was a twenty-two-year-old girl with a dark complexion and sharp facial features. She wore the usual ashram uniform: a red, white and orange saree, draped around her scrawny body.

Rigu introduced her with a warm tone. "Please welcome Kuntala. She is one among you, a sincere, hardworking disciple of this ashram. I am told she can read most comprehensive visions of the distant future. Her eyes have seen the happenings of the impending catastrophe with remarkable exactitude. Although there were a few missing pieces in her visions, other time-readers from the Bhavi group could fill them in. While she is the one speaking, she does so on the behalf of the collective effort of the whole Bhavi group. Kuntala, the stage is yours."

Rigu gave way for Kuntala to take the center-stage and sat on a chair nearby. He knew that Kuntala was going to give a detailed account of a sophisticated future. Much of the terminology she was going to use would have been incomprehensible to a common man of that age, but most in the audience were time-readers. They knew the future and had made their peace with the complexity of it.

Kuntala was sweating and her hands were shaky as she walked to the center of the rostrum. She carried a few pieces of paper in her hands. She gulped and started to read from the first page.

"Five thousand years into the future, on January 1st, 2069…"

"Speak louder, my child" Rigu interrupted her. "I am

sure your friends at the end cannot hear a word."

Kuntala cleared her throat and started again.

"Five thousand years into the future, on January 1st, 2069, Vedvance Technologies Inc., United States, will make a path-breaking announcement. They will present a technology which promises to change the course of human history forever.

"The executives from Vedvance Inc. will produce a much-anticipated press-release suggesting that after several years of biotech research, a singularity between human consciousness and artificial intelligence has finally been achieved. They will announce the retail availability of "Concordia VX." This device can be injected at the back of the neck with a simple injection. The device would then give the human brain complete access to a machine level intelligence. This singularity between man and machine will be an unparalleled feat of technology. This device will allow a human to enhance his or her intelligence, decision-making power, and reactionary instincts twenty times over those of a normal human being.

"They will also announce that their engineering team will send several regular updates and bug fixes over following few months. These remote updates will make Concordia VX even better, smarter and more integrated into the human brain."

So far, so good, Rigu thought. The vision was the same as the one presented to him a few weeks ago. Having listened to visions of the future multiple times, he had made it a mental habit to put mental markers on where exactly a vision changes.

"One week later, on January 8th, 2069, Vedvance Inc. will conduct a mega media-event in downtown Manhattan.

In this gala-event, they will activate Concordia VX remotely for three million customers. These customers would be the early bird buyers who pre-ordered the device and injected themselves with it in the previous few months. This event and further such events in the following years would be a huge success throughout the globe. This technology will go viral among the masses within no time. Within the next three to four years, this number of three million customers will rise to a massive 8.7 billion. Roughly 85% of the world population will have injected themselves with Concordia VX."

"When will Kumbh and Vetri enter this time-slice?" Rigu couldn't hold back any longer. "Has the date changed? Or the host bodies—is there a change there?"

"The date has not altered, but there is another major change, Gurudev. Earlier we could see both Kumbh and Vetri entering the year 2072, but now it's only Kumbh."

"Okay, that's good. Change is good—our efforts are making dents in the timeline. But when does Kumbh enter this timeline. Is there a change in the date?"

"No. Kumbh is first seen in this time-slice on November 19th, 2072, as was the case earlier."

"Ok. Please continue Kuntala." Rigu hid the look of disappointment on his face with a wry smile, which looked more like a frown. Kuntala continued.

"On November 19th, 2072, Kumbh will acquire a vessel by the name of Karlesha Breathnach, a child prodigy. This detail also matches our previous visions. Karlesha is a super-intellectual computer scientist and ethical hacker of German-Irish descent. She works as a post-graduate researcher with Fern-Maroll University's Center of Artificial Neural Networks. She is one of the lead algorithm designers and network programmers for the Concordia VX project. She stays in a city-area called North-West NYC. On this date, she will be exactly nineteen years, six months, and twenty-three days old."

"Same girl? Same Karlesha Breathnach? The same city?" Rigu murmured to himself in disbelief. "Are you sure, Kuntala? These details are exactly the same as your previous vision?"

"Yes, all these details are exactly the same as my earlier visions. I mean, our earlier visions."

"Go on. Describe the rest of the vision."

This was not looking good. They were so close to putting Kumbh and Vetri in the time-prison. Yet the future visions were not reflecting the changes Rigu was expecting.

Kuntala turned over the page. "Within a few minutes of possession, Kumbh will take over Karlesha's body completely. He will suppress her consciousness as time-demons do. She will slowly drop her regular schedule, shun her friends, her usual habits, and her work. She will lock herself in a small apartment complex at a desolate location. Through the intellectual skills of this vessel, Kumbh will soon set up himself on the dark-net cyberspace as a notorious hacker, *Trisillex Agneta*. He will then start hacking more than two million government and private websites within a span of one month. This mass cyber upheaval will send most of the global cyber-security authorities on wild-goose chases around the world."

Kuntala paused to look at the faces in the crowd. They were gazing at her in awe. She wiped the sweat on her forehead and continued.

"Trisillex will leave breadcrumbs and false identities throughout the cyber-space. This will create a muddle of electronic footprints and red herrings. Because of these, global police organizations will perceive it as a massive hacking conspiracy by a major group of hackers. On December 20th, 2072, as per Trisillex's well-laid setup, a joint team of Interpol and CIA, will arrest seventeen members of a group called "Paint Me Bleak Red,' a.k.a. PAMBLER. Trisillex would have meticulously framed PAMBLER for these cyber violations. In the spirit of swift justice, the captured members of PAMBLER will be sentenced to two thousand years in maximum-security prison by an NYC court. PAMBLER's head Vijuheet Baal, a.k.a. the Red Snake will be thrown in two years of solitary confinement before he begins his actual sentence. These arrests will bring the past few days of the manhunt and media questioning to rest.

"Security organizations will see this as a massive victory. Several officers will be commended and promoted. Medals of honor will be given out to numerous police personnel in elaborate ceremonies. Worldwide, the gatekeepers of cyber-crime will go into celebratory mode—completely unaware that a dark entity lurks in the virtual mesh."

Rigu was getting more restless, and the look of disappointment on his face was deepening. The dominant future had not changed at all, which was concerning.

"On the next day, December 21st, 2072, Trisillex will start hacking into the Vedvance's systems. Over the next few hours, he will gain access to critical security protocols and acquire admin account privileges. As the next step, he will disable all alarms and failsafe mechanisms within their systems, one by one. To stay under the radar, he will only spend time taking control, and not use that control at all. He will wait in stealth mode until he is completely ready for his final blow.

"At exactly 8:42 PM Eastern Time, December 22nd, 2072, Trisillex will finish acquiring complete control of Concordance VX servers. At 08:43 PM, he will quietly send system updates to the devices of all the 8.7 billion customers plugged into Concordance VX's Cloud. This Trojan horse update will be shown to users as a routine, automatic bug-fixing patch. Users will be cautioned that without this critical update, Concordia VX will slow down.

"But at the back-end, this code-patch will do a critical alteration in Concordia's core system. This update will secretly reverse the 'Human Over AI' HOA protocol. As per the original protocol design of Concordance VX devices, the human consciousness would have been able to supersede any of the Concordance A.I.'s commands. But this reversal will make sure that Concordance A.I.s can, in fact, override any of the human consciousness's commands—a protocol called the 'A.I. over Human' AOH protocol. And then, at 7:33 AM December 23rd, 2072, is when…I can't read any further." Kuntala's eyes were wet, her throat heavy with the sea of emotions scalding inside of her. She shuddered every time she re-imagined her horrific visions of the future.

"Kid, please? We need to hear it. We're working together to avert this future. So please go on." Rigu scowled.

Kuntala pressed her lips together and nodded. She was trying hard not to burst into tears. She hated revisiting it. But she had her orders.

"At 7:33 AM, on December 23rd, 2072, Kumbh a.k.a Trisillex will send a message to each of the 8.7 billion Concordance devices. This message will instruct the

A.I. to immediately suspend every possible physiological function of its host body. The message would otherwise have been ignored by the HOA protocol. Each of the devices will send strong electric waves to the host brain. These electric charges will fry large parts of the cerebrum, thalamus, and brain stem from within for each host.

"Billions of souls will drop dead to the ground within a matter of few seconds. Parents, children, policemen, leaders, caregivers—all annihilated within a few moments. Numerous vehicles, trains, and planes being manned by human pilots and drivers will crash into each other or into surrounding buildings. This will cause fires, pillage, and even more devastation. A major part of human life on Earth will be wiped out from a single stroke of Kumbh's evil plan. Our planet will experience a large-scale near-extinction event—without a single drop of blood being shed." Tears rolled down Kuntala's cheeks, and she sobbed.

A feeling of gloom spread on the crowd. Several of them had tears in their eyes. Many of them sat on their knees, feeling weak down to their guts. They were men and women who had seen a lot of vehement bloodied wars and conquests through their time visions. But such a gigantic loss of life in a fraction of seconds was difficult to comprehend.

Rigu stood up and gently placed her hand on Kuntala's head. He signaled for her to return to her place and then addressed the crowd.

"This is the ghastly future we have been fighting to avoid, my children. Hopefully, after we throw Kumbh and Vetri into the time-prison today, the future will change. If that happens, billions of lives will not be lost.

Hope is all we have, and our best efforts are what we can do."

Day 1 of 7

4
KUMBH'S ESTRANGED SON

he year was 3057 BC. Twenty years had gone by since that fateful night when Rigu saved the lives of the mother-son duo. Tej was now a full-grown man with the sturdy frame of a farmer, and the instincts of a trained athlete. After the incident in the Dandak forest, Tej and his mother had stayed in Rigu's ashram for a few days. Rigu had sent them to a village called Sarp-nagar. A village couple gave them a place to stay, and they had been living there since.

Five years ago, Tej was also united in wedlock to a girl, Damayanti, and had a sweet four-year-old daughter, Kaalpriya. Three years ago, his mother had died a peaceful death in her sleep. When that happened, he felt as if his whole world was destroyed—as if a part of him was lost forever. He stopped eating and cried for days. No one was able to console him. But the sun still rose every-day and brightened the sky. The raindrops still fell, and the crops still bore grain. The world moved on, and he did, too.

One afternoon, Tej was sitting in his circular bamboo hut, whittling a small wooden log with a sharp knife. This was his cozy workshop, where he worked for hours on end. He spent time fixing his farming equipment and building and sharpening new bows and arrows for his crop-protection duties.

This hut was around ten feet tall, and the bamboo sticks composing the walls were painted dark brown with a special dense dye made from a wild-fruit. A few knives of various sizes hung on the wall facing him. Two equipment-sharpening limestones were kept at one side. Although there was some clutter in the room, the whole place had an austere ambiance.

Next to Tej sat his new friend, Manu Kumar, another farmer's son. Tej was teaching Manu how to build a bow and an arrow from scratch. His efforts were in vain, as Manu had rarely used weapons.

"When you are tying a string to a bow, dear Manu, you must not let go of the other end of the bow. Otherwise, you cannot tie a string to the bow. You are my age; you should have been a trained archer and swordsman by now. But you are not even a novice," Tej taunted.

"So what? With you as my guru, I will learn within a few months." Manu smiled.

"A few months? No, no, you have to learn in a few days. Your family is new to the village, and your parents don't know the rules here. All able-bodied villagers have to engage in specific harvest-related activities. The first few weeks were fine—your family was new, and was given time to learn our ways. But soon, the members of your family, including you, will have community duties ascribed to you."

"Community duties?" Manu's eyes stretched wide

with bewilderment. Anything related to a duty or hard work was akin to punishment to him.

"Yes. The village headman will assign the next round of farm protection duty in a few days. If your name comes up for volunteering, how will you protect our cattle and our crops from wild animals? With a wooden stick? No. You will have to scare the wild animals off with sharp arrows, wound them, or even kill them if required. But the first step to being an archer is to learn to tie a string to a bow. That's a basic," Tej explained to Manu as if teaching a small child.

As Tej took the untied bow from Manu's hands, their hands touched for a moment, and they both felt a bit awkward.

"I didn't mean to touch you. I'm sorry," Tej said. He gulped with guilt.

"It's all right, brother, no problem." Manu wanted this odd moment to be over.

"Don't call me brother. I've told you many times," Tej responded with slight anger in his tone.

"I am sorry, Tej. So you were going to tell me to tie the bow. Teach me, please. I heard you have killed many panthers that once haunted these woods." Manu changed the topic.

Seeing Manu smile, Tej quelled himself and looked at him with an affectionate gaze. "Yeah, I did slay a panther once and hurt another. But don't worry. I will definitely teach you. In fact, I won't rest until you are the best archer in the whole kingdom. Even if we have to spend countless hours here or in the field, practicing."

There was a knock on the door. Tej's daughter Kaalpriya came in and hugged him from the side. She wore a flower-patterned pink dress and a little metal necklace. Two small anklets of matching designs decorated her tiny feet. Her well-oiled and plaited hair was neatly tied at the back. When she smiled, the spaces between her teeth were visible. Tej smiled and kissed her forehead.

"Baba, an old man is here. He is looking for you," she whispered in Tej's ear, but spoke the last word loudly, and tittered.

"Old man? Where is he?"

"He is also coming here. I challenged him to race with me and see if I came first."

And then Guru Rigu entered the workshop. Tej felt serendipitous. It had been twenty years since he'd met the guru.

Rigu looked as if he hadn't aged a bit. If he had, it was too difficult for Tej to determine. Both Tej and Manu Kumar paused for a moment. They then jumped to their feet and placed their foreheads at the sage's feet with respect. Rigu smiled and blessed them.

Manu Kumar quipped, "I'll come later, Tej," and ran out of the hut. Tej gestured for Kaalpriya to also go outside, but she refused to do so. Tej gave her a look of feigned anger, and she ran outside, jumping and chirping. Tej cleaned a small bamboo chair in haste and offered the sage to take a seat.

"It's been a long time, Tej. How have you been? Do you even remember me?" Rigu sat on the chair, and Tej sat near the guru's feet.

"How could I forget you, Gurudev? You were the savior who not only extricated us from the clutches of death but also sent us to this beautiful village. This calm, peaceful abode has nurtured us ever since. My foster parents have been such kind souls, who helped my mother take care of me. In this sanctuary, she was able to raise me the way she wanted to—away from the shadow of evil."

"So I see. You are grown up and well taken care of. She raised you right."

"I am what I am because of her. Even though those years of torment devastated her, she showered so much love on me that I could get past those days of terror."

Tej wiped a tear from his eye. His mother's death had created a void in his otherwise contented life, which he felt he could never fill. "Mother spoke of you with high regard, Gurudev. If she were alive today, she would have been elated to see you. But she left us three years ago. Did you hear that news? You would have—I forgot you are a time-reader. You know many things." Tej blurted out those words in one go as if he had been practicing them forever.

"You say you have heard so much about me from your mother, yet you never paid a visit to me in my ashram?" Rigu lovingly taunted Tej.

"The thought of visiting you crossed my mind a few times, Gurudev, but how could I? That night, that jungle. For me, they symbolized the torture me and mother had to endure for years. As a kid that day, I saw the talons of death so close, yet I felt so helpless. If you had not arrived at that moment, we would not have been alive. Even today, I shudder to think of our impending fate.

"I can't go near that forest, ever. I hate that part of my life and wish to forget it completely. Unfortunately, I can't. To this day, I get frequent nightmares, in which I live through that night again and again. I see myself and my mother being chased and threatened. Those demons— their faces are so clear. I wish they were in front of me. I would have crushed their skulls with my bare hands, and would have thrown away their flesh and bones for wild animals to devour." Tej's face went red with anger. His eyes were bloodshot, and his body trembled with rage.

Rigu looked at Tej and took a deep breath. "Those are not mere nightmares, Tej. Every time you think you are seeing those specters from past, you are actually going back in time and visiting that particular night."

Tej couldn't understand what Rigu meant.

Rigu continued. "Owing to the trauma you experienced, your consciousness is anchored to that night. It keeps time-traveling to that moment, especially when you are between your weak sleep and deep sleep stages. That is when your body's hold on your consciousness is the weakest. Whenever you do go back, you can't enter any of the human bodies, but I believe your consciousness is entering other small organisms, insects, frogs. I am not sure which ones."

"What are you saying, Gurudev? I am traveling in time? How can I do that? Some of these dreams do feel vivid and intense. But dreams usually appear real when we are in them. That happens with most people, right?"

"I know it's a lot to take, Tej. But you have the same ability those demons had. Your consciousness can crawl through time and enter other humans or living organisms. You, Tej … are a time-demon."

Tej was stunned.

"But Gurudev, how can I be a time-demon? How can I have these powers? I have been studying ancient texts since I was a child. Lore says that the time-demons obtained these powers as boons only after they engaged in years of worship in the name of Goddess Trikaaldevi. How could I have the power of time travel without doing any of that holy penance?"

"All those are just scriptures, Tej, stories for gullible minds. Time-travel was actually a crucial step in human evolution. There were many times in the past when the human species were completely wiped out from the face of the earth. The only humans that survived these apocalypses were the time-travelers. They moved their consciousnesses out of human bodies before the cataclysms hit the planet. Hence they survived the doomsday, every time."

"And where did they go?"

"They moved to future times when humanoid civilizations again prospered on earth. Without them, the post-apocalyptic people would have started from scratch. But previous knowledge accumulated by these time travelers helped mankind make giant strides at a fast pace. Messiahs, saviors, many of the ancient leaders were actually time-travelers. They 'reincarnated' themselves again and again over the ages, and led humanity on the righteous path."

"That sounds like a good deed, Gurudev. I never knew this. But if they were the righteous leaders, why are they called time-demons?"

"While some of these time travelers worked for the welfare of humanity, many of them started abusing these powers. Driven by their animalistic needs, they traveled back and forth in time. With each journey, they possessed human beings with power, wealth, and the means to rule over others. This act of forceful possession of other bodies earned them the name 'time-demons.'"

"But you said I'm a time-demon, too? How is that possible? I have never traveled through time. How am I a part of this evolution?" This was too far-fetched for

Tej to believe.

Rigu went silent. He closed his eyes as if doing a careful evaluation of what to say next. What he was about to tell Tej was a damning life-altering fact. He opened his eyes after a few moments and asked, "Are you sure you are ready for the truth, Tej? Truth is like that bitter drink which looks appealing when in the glass, but when ingested, only brings pain and sorrow."

"What truth? Tell me, Gurudev."

"You have obtained these powers via your genes. You have these powers because you are Kumbh's son."

5
NEUROTOXIN IN THY BLOODSTREAM

Tej gulped the bile of anger down his throat. For the past twenty years of his life, he had been thinking of a thousand different ways for how he would kill Kumbh and Vetri one day, and exact his sweet revenge. But today, he'd learned that one devil was, in fact, his father. He was not sure what to feel anymore.

He spoke through a clogged throat. "Mother never told me that. She usually avoided talking about my father. She said Kumbh and Vetri killed him when I was a toddler."

"She had her reasons, Tej."

"Tell me more, Gurudev." Tej lowered his head and closed his eyes, feeling cheated.

"Time-demons such as Kumbh and Vetri maintain huge harems full of humans. They kept men and women as sex slaves. Your mother ran from one such harem that night. Since the time-demons sexually exploited the women in the harem, they also had to devise ways to avoid progeny so that their seed didn't take root within a slave. Kumbh and Vetri, being the ruthless savages they were, had equally cruel methods to prevent pregnancy among their slaves."

"I have vivid memories of that place, that harem, Gurudev. Those remembrances haunt my dreams to this today. But I don't remember their particular ways."

"Your brain did the right thing by repressing most of those negative memories. Their acts were indeed reprehensible. Their harem-keeper servants administered snake-poison to the women on a periodic basis. Quantities were small enough to keep the women alive but large enough to keep their bodies frail and prevent any life from germinating in them. The miracle is that despite the regular intake of that toxin, your mother not only got impregnated with you but also gave birth successfully."

"Why did they not kill me while I was in her womb, or at birth?"

"Your mother was a courageous lady who fought not only for herself but for other slaves, too. Kumbh and Vetri could have killed you right when they knew she was carrying you. But she begged for your life and agreed to comply with their demands without protesting, which she always did otherwise. They figured they would keep you alive as leverage against her, and kill you any day when they felt it appropriate. But fate was weaving a different tale. Your mother escaped with you and came to Dandak Forest that night. Unassisted, Kumbh and Vetri came running after her, and I could capture those demons."

A thousand feelings went through Tej's mind like waves in a turbulent ocean. He felt as if his whole life has been a lie. He had a faint memory of Kumbh's harem and his private bacchanalian ceremonies. Only now could he understand how difficult those days must have been for his mother. She'd sacrificed her dignity, her persona, her whole life, to keep him alive.

He felt rage building within him. All the animosities he had been nurturing against the time-demons had been re-invigorated. He noticed Rigu looking at him as if reading his deliberations.

"Gurudev, if I'm a time-demon too, then please tell me—how can I use this power? I want to go back in time to a moment before you captured those demons so that I can have my revenge."

"Revenge?" Rigu raised one of his eyebrows a little.

"Yes, Gurudev. I have been training for my whole life. Archery, swordsmanship—I can fight two swordsmen at once. I can shoot a running target from several hundred feet away. These proficiencies were not useful for me as a farmer. But even so, I mastered them. I have been waiting for the moment when I will seek my vengeance. Please help me take my consciousness into the body of an able warrior in the past. I will confront those bastards and teach them a lesson that other evil savages will remember for ages."

"The universe has granted your wish, Tej. Soon, you will have a chance to exact your revenge—though not in the way you are thinking. The reason I am here is that Kumbh has escaped the time-prison where I captured him twenty years ago. We need to put him back where he belongs once again.

"Uncountable innocent lives are in danger because of what he is planning to do in the future. I need all the help I can get to stop him. In fact, while I was traveling from my ashram to your village, I was thinking about this meeting with you, deliberating on how I'd have to motivate you to help me re-capture Kumbh. But after talking to you, I am sure you are ready to commit yourself for this battle already."

"I am at your service, Gurudev." Tej folded his hands in respect. "But Vetri? Where is he? I want to cut those hands of his, which touched my mother."

"That's the primary reason I came to you, Tej. Vetri could not travel through time after that night. When you bit his wrist that night, you released a powerful neurotoxin in his bloodstream. It's strange that the toxin did no harm to his host body. But it changed the fundamental constituent structure of the host brain. After that night, his consciousness remained trapped within that host. He tried to escape, but couldn't."

"I released some kind of venom his bloodstream?"

"Yes, you did. When you and your mother stayed at my ashram, I drew several blood samples from yourself and your mother. It was your blood that showed the presence of this neurotoxin."

Tej slapped himself three or four times as if struggling to wake up from a dream, and Rigu chuckled. "No, Tej, this is not a dream."

"It feels like one, Gurudev. First, you've visited me after so many years. You tell me I am a time-demon. Besides that, you also say that Kumbh is my father. And I also had a toxin in my blood which somehow entrapped Vetri in his body after I bit him?"

"I must apologize, Tej. I wanted to tell you these facts at the right time and at a much slower pace. But Kumbh's escape has pushed my timeline."

"Please don't apologize, Gurudev. I have a lot of faith in your decisions. You know the best. Tell me more about this toxin in my body."

"This is not a normal toxin, Tej. Any toxin which acts on consciousness has to first reach the brain. For that, it has to cross the endothelial cells—that is, the blood-brain barrier, which only allows specific materials to pass through, and is almost impenetrable. Your toxin could cheat this impenetrable barrier, too, which is unheard of in this time-slice. Only scientists of the future would be able to build medicines bio-engineered to permeate this membrane. Despite my extensive research on time-demons, I cannot explain this phenomenon. But I have kept Vetri's body in my ashram, under a dose of heavy anesthetics. He stays entrapped in there forever."

"This is hard to stomach, Gurudev. How can I release a neurotoxin through my teeth? How did I get this poison in my body in the first place?"

"You are forgetting that you not only germinated within your mother but thrived as a fetus, despite the fact that those beasts were giving small doses of snake poison to her periodically. Your anatomy was not only resistant to that snake-poison but also blossomed within its lethal environment. You were born with traces of that poison within your body. And since your antibodies formed later, they did not treat those poisonous substances as foreign objects. During eight years of your upbringing, that simple snake-poison underwent biological magnification. It turned into a potent neurotoxin. That's the venom which you injected into him that day. An eight-year-old child, you brought down mighty Vetri with a venom-bite. Now that you are twenty-eight, I am curious how pernicious that venom would be today."

Tej felt a bit awkward. Was he some kind of a snake-man? He had heard parables of men and women who were called snake-people. Their bites had the same murderous potency as of a poisonous snake.

"I haven't ever felt I am a toxic person—though a venomous snake bit me when I was fifteen years old, and nothing happened to me. I have seen people dying within a few moments after those snake-bites, yet I was unharmed. I believed that something was wrong with me. Otherwise, why was I not affected by that lethal sting? Hence, I kept the incident to myself. I suppose the virulent poison which flows in my veins protected me."

"Yes, it did. And I don't believe your toxin is poisonous to humans. But it has a definite entrapping impact on other time-demons."

Rigu realized a lot of time had passed since they began talking. He stood up and looked outside the window, at the sunlight, gauging the time of the day.

"We will discuss more later, Tej. For now, we need to chart out a strategy to capture Kumbh as soon as possible. Time is of the essence because we have less than seven days. But before we do anything, I want to get you ready for this battle. Once we capture Kumbh's consciousness in his old body, we will administer your poison to him. As a result, he will be imprisoned inside that vessel forever. That's the best punishment for him."

Tej looked at Rigu. He was still trying to make sense of what the Guru had said. The sage coming to him one fine day, after twenty years' absence, and loading him with the phantasmal memories from the past, was too much for him to take in.

Rigu, who could somehow decipher Tej's dissonant thoughts, smiled.

"I know you have many questions, Tej. Myself coming here one day and dragging you into a strange conflict is overwhelming for you. But I wouldn't have come to you if it was not of the utmost urgency. I assure you that in due course, you will have your answers."

"There's one more thing I wanted to tell you, Gurudev." Tej could not find the right words to convey what he wanted to say. Mentioning something like this to a respected sage and his guardian angel was difficult for him. He was drowning in his own guilt. Words started in his throat but skipped his tongue.

"Gurudev, actually, I have…" Tej stammered.

"You have feelings of affection towards Manu Kumar. Isn't it true, Tej?" Rigu looked into Tej's eyes as if navigating through his soul.

"Yes, that is true. I know I am not supposed to like another man. It's unnatural. That, too, when I already have a devoted wife and a lovely daughter. But I am attracted to him. In fact, I usually liked the boys around me, more than I liked the girls. I didn't want to get married. But when my foster parents found Damayanti for me, I could not say no to them."

Tej weighed his words and spoke again. "Manu Kumar came to our village only a few months ago. But ever since he came, I want to spend more and more time only with him. Why do I have these unnatural feelings? These abnormal desires make me feel that I have sinned. How could a reprobate such as me fight by your side in this holy battle?"

Tej felt a ton of weight lifted off his shoulders as he spoke those words. Given the societal pressure, he had never confessed his sexual inclination to anyone until today—not even his mother, to whom he was very close. But today in front of Rigu, he somehow could not contain this secret anymore.

"Tej, for my whole life, I have been reading time. I have seen the past, the present, and the future. I have realized that there is only one sin in this whole world—that is to hurt another living being, who means you no harm, through your direct or indirect intentional actions. So your feelings are not sinful.

"There were times in the past, and there will be times in future when men liking men, and women liking women, will be an acceptable social practice. But unfortunately for you, today in this age and in this realm, it's not. So let go of your guilt. You have committed no sin. I am sure that you will keep fulfilling your duties as a sincere husband and as a loving father. Discard these doubts. I want your head completely in the game. This is the most crucial battle we will ever fight for humanity. So get ready, and say your goodbyes. We need to travel to my ashram right away."

There was some kind of magic in Rigu's reassuring words, and they rejuvenated Tej. He felt his guilt and gloominess slipping away. The fire of vengeance was burning inside of him, unabated. "I am ready for this battle, Gurudev. Please, tell me—when do I get to go to the past and fight with Kumbh?"

"Not to the past, Tej. The future. Kumbh is in the future."

6

VIRTUAL EXOSKELETON, VIRTEXO 2.0

few minutes later, Tej had a heated argument with his wife Damayanti. Tej assured her he would be back in a few days, but he did not reveal the details of his discussion with Rigu.

She could not understand the reason behind his sudden plans to travel. She fought, she cried, but then made her peace. She knew Tej. She knew once he decided to do something, he rarely rested before hitting his mark. He was stubborn that way. She packed a bag of clothes for his journey.

Tej said his goodbyes to his foster parents, to his friends, and to Manu Kumar. He told them that he was visiting Guru Rigu's ashram for a few days of meditation and relaxation.

As he was about to leave, Kaalpriya came running to him.

"When will you come back, Baba?"

"Very soon, kiddo."

"Why can't I come with you?"

"I explained that to you a few minutes back. Right? If you come with me, then how will you play near the river? There is no river where I am going."

"Okay. But if you come back and I am grown up, how will you recognize me?" The child had tears in her eyes. Her face had turned pink.

"I will be back soon. Don't you cry now. Otherwise, how will I leave? You're my strong kiddo. Right?"

Kaalpriya removed a small red glass bangle from her wrist and gave it to Tej. "Take my bangle with you. Ma says my face is round like this bangle is. If you look at this every day, you will remember my face."

Tej hugged her tightly. Tears rolled down his cheeks. He had no words

Rigu's Ashram | A Few Hours Later

Rigu arrived at his ashram with Tej. After getting refreshed, they were sitting and talking in a quiet, austere room made of fire-torched mud bricks. Tej drank a hot liquid from a small earthen pot mug. Rigu was explaining to Tej the intricacies of traveling through time. Tej listened attentively. The hot liquid he was drinking was a soothing medicine, which, according to Rigu, would prepare him for his travel through time.

"Tej, you have some inkling of time travel. Now I will discuss with you the concept of a time-prison. These details may not make a lot of sense to you, but I will lay them out in simple words. You need to understand these theories and embrace this knowledge at a swift pace. It will be critical for our success in this battle."

"I am ready, Gurudev. Wherever I have questions, I will ask them."

"Good. Since a time-demon's consciousness can travel through time, I had to capture Kumbh in a Kaal-Shoonya. The literal translation of Kaal-Shoonya is Time-nothingness. It's a space where the concept of time does not exist. Roughly around five thousand years in the future, humans will develop such a place, a virtual-reality based multiplayer game called "Virtual Exoskeleton 2.0" or *Virtexo* 2.0. This game will allow human beings to enter into that virtual reality and, in a phony way, lead a life very different from their true life."

"Pardon my ignorance, Gurudev. What is a virtual-reality?"

"How will I explain this to you? Okay. You do understand dreams. Think of virtual reality as an artificial construct, a well-crafted dream—a reverie which allows a human to experience several fantastical worlds without actually traveling to them."

"So, virtual reality is a dream which humans will create? But how?" Tej was puzzled, but not defeated, by the logic of what he was hearing.

"Using machines, like the bow and arrow. A bow and arrow is a very simple instrument, a rudimentary machine which you can use to hunt animals. The humans of the future will have far more sophisticated machines which can fabricate these dreams, and in a way, put human consciousness within them."

Rigu knew he'd used a loose analogy, but Tej understood the underlying philosophy.

"Okay, Gurudev, so what you are saying is that Kumbh was imprisoned in that dream, and that dream has no concept of time?"

"Yes, I am coming to that. So within that game Virtexo 2.0, there are different stages. Think of these stages as steps or levels of a ladder. Within each stage, the game players win over some milestones and keep on moving forward to following levels."

"Okay!"

"There was one stage of this game which the game developers left unfinished. Hence, in that stage, the concept of time was not introduced. But within this stage, they had created a virtual character called *Mengalz*. This is the virtual character within which I captured Kumbh's consciousness."

"Captured? I don't understand."

"On that night, when we brought them to my ashram, Kumbh woke up from the effect of my paralytic chemical after a few hours. He was in a delirious state. As a natural time-demon instinct, he wanted to take flight. He wanted to move his consciousness from that body to another, right away. Exactly at that time, I showed him a well-drawn sketch of Mengalz, which worked as a hint to his destination. In that state of disorientation, his judgment was weak. He transported his consciousness to that virtual character. But once he went into that game, inside the body of that character, it became his prison. He no longer had any time waves to ride on and get out."

"I am not sure I understand very well, Gurudev. But you are saying you tricked him in going to that time-prison, is that right?" Tej had concluded that it was not possible for him to understand each word the guru was saying or will say. But he planned to pick-up the parts which he could understand.

"Yes, I tricked him. Exactly."

"But how did he even take your bait? He is one of the most powerful time-demons, known throughout history."

"He is. But most time-demons function on the concept of anchor and destination. A time-demon, when planning a jump through time, needs to establish his or her anchor. An anchor is the current host body to which they are tethered, as well as the current time realm they are in.

"Along with this anchor, they also need to establish a destination host body and time-slice to select. When Kumbh woke up, his consciousness was searching for destination bodies in other time-slices. At that time, a mere suggestion of 2024 AD and a sketch of that character Mengalz worked as a hint to his consciousness.

"As soon as he entered Virtexo, inside the character of Mengalz, he could not travel any further. He was trapped there, because that stage of the game, there was no time." Rigu finished his explanation and noticed that Tej was scratching his head in confusion.

"Will all due respect, Gurudev, I am not sure if I understood each word you said. But two words stay with me—anchor and destination."

"Yes, and those two words are critical for you, Tej. These two concepts will aid you to travel to far destinations. They will also help you anchor back to your source using the time-tether."

Rigu opened the large wooden box near the window and took out several sketches which he'd made a few years ago. The sketches were drawn on thick sheets of paper. In places, they were shaded with different colored powders and charcoal.

Few sketches described the night Rigu captured

Kumbh and Vetri. Few other drawings showed fantastical futuristic images of Virtexo. Some had various game-characters in strange clothes. The character of Mengalz looked like a small boy. The boy had yellow hair, a big nose, broken teeth, and wore a red shirt with blue jeans. In a weird way, it reminded Tej of Kaalpriya. He was already missing her.

Tej found some of the sketches bizarre but took a detailed look at them. While going through them, he recalled a fact Rigu had mentioned earlier.

"There is one thing I didn't understand, Gurudev. You said we only have seven days before we can capture Kumbh? What is the logic behind that?"

"Yes, Tej, today at 6 PM Eastern time in 2024 AD …"

"Eastern?"

"Oh, I keep forgetting you don't see what I can see. This morning, sometime around sunrise our time, Virtexo's development team uploaded a code-fix to the game. This fix introduced the concept of time in the stage of the game where Mengalz, i.e. Kumbh, was entrapped. At that exact instant, Kumbh re-gained his powers and moved his consciousness out of that game character. He acquired a new host, a human within the same time-slice—that is, in 2024 AD. At that moment, I intercepted a great shock-wave traveling through time. I realized that Kumbh has broken free of the time jail, which is when I rushed to your village."

"So that's how he escaped."

"Yes. And this escape would not have been possible without external intervention. If this escape was pre-destined, we would have seen it earlier in our time visions. Anything in the future which does not involve time-demons is crystal-clear to us. We can see it whenever we want, and it will remain the same. But the situations affected by time-demon actions only reveal themselves as they take those actions—which is why I am sure that in this case, another time-demon helped him escape."

"But where do seven days come into the picture?" Tej was rather flummoxed with these theories, characters, and the concept of time-prison.

"I am coming to that. When I entrapped Kumbh into Virtexo twenty years ago, he lost touch with time. His anchor location was cut off. As a result of this, he will be stuck in the year 2024 for seven days. He will not be able to travel to another time-slice right away.

"Time-demon's anchors are rarely severed like this because they are consistently traveling through time. But when a time-demon's anchor is cut off for some reason, he needs approximately seven days of time, to reestablish it. He has to spend those seven days to re-build the current location and time as a new anchor. Only after the completion of these seven days can he make the next time jump to a new destination."

"Oh, so these are the seven days you were talking about."

"Yes—after today's sunrise, we have seven days before he makes his next time jump. After the sunset of the seventh day, he will be free to make a fresh time jump at any time. With this reestablished anchor, he will go farther in the future, where he will be beyond our reach. We need to capture him right where he currently is, in the year 2024 AD."

"Okay, Gurudev. Let us for a moment assume that I can somehow go to this 2024, to the future. I find him, and I am even able to somehow capture him. But how will we bring his consciousness to our current time? He may move to a new body at any time, and I will have to go looking for his new vessel?"

"No, he can't move to another body right away, because his anchor is weakened. That's our advantage. When I send your consciousness to a body in 2024, you will need to find him and look into his eyes."

"Look into his eyes? Why?"

"Although his anchor is severed, the remnants of his previous anchor are still connected to his consciousness. As soon as you look into his eyes, his consciousness will read your consciousness's anchor. And that anchor lies in the present time, i.e. 3057 BC. His consciousness will re-establish its anchor to yours. That, Tej, will be your advantage. After that as soon as you travel back to this time, you will drag his consciousness along."

Tej chewed his lower lip and looked at Rigu as if he was a child about to be reprimanded by his teacher. He had not understood a single word of what the guru said. He only gathered that he could somehow travel through time and go to some future, and once he got there, he needed to find Kumbh and look into his eyes.

"Please pardon me, Gurudev. These concepts are too confusing for me. First, I don't know how to travel through time to the future. And second, when I go and visit him in the future, why should I look into his eyes? Why shouldn't I kill him there and then, and end his life forever?"

Rigu knew that time was running out and Tej's questions were too basic. But he also knew that if Tej was not prepared in the right way, this whole undertaking could be rendered futile. Too much depended on Tej's success.

He placed his hands on Tej's shoulders. "Son, do you

trust me?"

"I do."

"Will you do exactly as I say? Will you fight this demon for me?"

"I owe my life to you, Gurudev. I would follow you to the end of the world if I have to. That night, when we had lost all hope, you were our light, and you were our savior."

"Good. Then you will follow my simple instructions as I guide you to where you have to go. Now, coming to your question about killing him. Please understand that time-demons cannot be killed in the same sense as humans can be. Time-demons are parasitic energies, pure consciousnesses. They own a host and tie themselves to it. Even if you kill Kumbh, i.e. Kumbh's host body in 2024 AD, you will only be killing that vessel. After his vessel dies, his consciousness will again travel to another vessel in 2024. And as the seventh day passes, he will be gone forever. So don't think too much on that.

"And about your doubts on your capability for time travel, please understand that it has been passed onto you via genetics. It's deep-rooted into your consciousness, too. It will come as easily to you as wielding a sword. Since you are a genetic time-demon, even if your consciousness leaves your body, it will stay hale and hearty until you come back. So if you can't trust yourself for now, please trust me. Because I chose you for a reason."

"All right, Gurudev, I will follow your instructions. But we have lost one day—the sun is about to set. We have only six days."

"Yes, we have lost this one day. But this one day was important for you to understand this situation, and to discuss and plan our path forward. Take a proper rest tonight. Tomorrow, you need to spend time learning another important skill—but not here; it will be at another place. You will need to learn how to conduct a *Pret-Baadha*, i.e. how to cast a spell and summon a demonic consciousness."

"Pret-Baadha? Why, and who will teach me?"

"To capture Kumbh's consciousness, you will have to look into his eyes. I told you that a few moments ago, right?"

"Yes—that's the only part I understood, Gurudev."

"So before you look into Kumbh's eyes, you would need to summon his consciousness, in the same way, any demon is summoned. Only after you run this pret-baadha spell will you be able to connect to Kumbh's consciousness. It's akin to a spell to cure demonic possession."

"Demonic possession?" Tej gulped in fear. He remembered seeing a dark shadow near his farm one night. He stayed as far away from it as possible. Village elders later told him it was the ghost of a farmer who was killed by wolves ten years ago. That has been his closest encounter with anything supernatural.

Rigu could understand his fear. "Don't worry, son. You will be taught by best of the best—Rudrakshini, the queen of necromancers."

Necromancer? Tej's eyes widened at the mere mention of the word. He had heard strange necromancer stories from his foster parents and community elders. In his village, people addressed necromancers as Aghori. They called Aghoris to perform exorcisms on village men or women who were claimed to be possessed by evil spirits.

He also had a vivid memory from childhood when he'd witnessed an exorcism live. Fifteen years ago an old Aghori was called in his village to exorcize a spirit. The subject was a man in his early twenties. This man started behaving in an erratic manner one day. He was found uttering strange words, making weird noises, and scratching his body. He fought with anyone who tried to come near him.

The Aghori came in and built a small bonfire. He then applied a thick paste on the subject's forehead. He touched his own forehead to the subject's forehead and started his incantation. Within a few minutes, the subject became normal. It was no less than a miracle.

The Aghori left with a mysterious smile on his face. Tej could never forget that uncanny smile. Those red, stained teeth, shining between those thin darkened lips, were too bizarre for him to forget. After that, Tej stayed away from the strange necromancy ceremonies.

"What are you saying, Gurudev? These people, these necromancers claim that they can talk to dead people. They deal with ghosts and ghouls. They engage in gory activities—like cannibalism and bathing in blood. Staying and eating on funeral grounds is common for them. Do you believe in their cult and philosophy?"

Rigu understood the deep prejudice Tej had for the discipline of necromancy. He felt it was important to remove this misconception right away.

"Tej, necromancy is another path to actualize yourself. Their ways are unusual, look different and darker. Their practices may appear strange and abhorrent. But their destination is the same: the pursuit of truth. Some of their practices are very scientific and are rooted deeply in reason and logic. I don't believe in following their cult, but I respect them as parallel pursuant of the same cause.

"Though I agree there are some quacks among their

ranks who don't have true power. These swindlers are masters of smokes and mirrors. They have corroded the name of the necromancy as a practice.

"But Rudrakshini was different. She was a prevailing necromancer and an eminent neuroscientist. The pastes, potions, and medical practices she mastered and documented are still used for curing several neurological disorders. Unfortunately, she is not known for these accomplishments. She is famous because she mastered the art of controlling consciousnesses. Controversial fields of study, such as astral-projection, reanimation, and posthumous-communication, which are shunned by researchers as pseudo-science, were pioneered by her. After her death, the necromancy cult has degenerated."

"Wait, Gurudev, is she dead?"

"Yes, she died three hundred years ago. But she is a legend. Several necromancer tribes still worship her like a queen mother, a goddess."

"But if she is dead, how will she teach me? We can't go to the past and…oh, okay."

"I can't go to the past. But you can. You are a time-demon!" Rigu smiled and stroked the back of Tej's head.

"Now have some food, son, and get a good sleep. We will begin before sunrise tomorrow, and we need to work a lot before you travel three hundred years in the past to Rudrakshini's lair."

Day 2 of 7

7

THE CHAMBER
OF TIME TRAVEL

he sun was about to rise. Rigu had woken up Tej early and asked him to get ready at once. They sat near the riverside, where the guru lit the holy fire and chanted several mantras. He also made Tej drink regular sips of water from a metal pot. Then he took Tej to a big, rectangular cottage with a slanting metal roof. This chamber was readied for Tej's travel through time.

Upon entering the chamber, Tej realized that the lights inside the chamber were dim. There were no windows, either. Only a few thick candles, kept on the ground near the walls, were illuminating the whole space. Another peculiar aspect of this chamber was that it was much bigger on the inside than it appeared from the outside. This was puzzling for Tej. The walls of the room were painted deep yellow, and with a red powder, long stripes of strange ancient symbols were smeared on them. It was unlike any room he had ever been in. The strange ambiance was making him even more nervous.

Guru signaled him to move further inside the room.

"Go on, Tej."

As Tej walked towards further into the room, what he saw impeded his steps and froze his blood. His nervousness turned into pure fear. He saw three huge rectangular cement blocks stationed at the center of the room in parallel. They sat approximately two meters apart from each other. On two of those blocks were two bodies bound in thick metal chains. Tej had recognized them as the bodies of Kumbh and Vetri. Kumbh's body was lying on the middle block; Vetri was on the left one. The block on the right was empty. That was for Tej.

"Tej, this concrete block is the physical anchor-pod for your upcoming travel. Lie down on this. In fact, this whole room has been prepped for time travelers to embark upon their voyages with ease."

"What are these big, strange symbols on the walls, Gurudev?" Tej asked as he placed himself on the cold cement block. He tried hard to deflect his mind away from the huge muscular bodies of time-demons lying next to him.

Rigu explained. "These symbols are part of a special warding done to keep other time-demon consciousnesses out of this sacred chamber. When you travel out from this time-slice to other time slices, your body, your vessel, will be empty. An empty body is an ideal space to make a home for evil souls looking for an entry in the physical world. These warding symbols ensure that no other evil entity can enter this room while you are gone. As an extra security precaution, I will surround this cement block with a thick layer of salt after you go. Salt keeps nefarious spirits at bay."

Tej gulped. "But these two bodies?"

"DON'T think about these bodies!" Rigu snapped.

Tej was taken aback by the Guru's sudden outburst. "I am sorry, Gurudev. I did not mean to—"

"Tej, listen to me carefully. I had prepared this room for easing the commencement of time travel. Forty-two learned priests sat here and chanted twenty thousand mantras addressing Goddess Trikaaldevi. They did so for fourteen days, praying and requesting her to bless this chamber. Inside this space, you have to be watchful of what you think.

"If you keep on thinking about these bodies of Kumbh and Vetri, your consciousness may be transported to the same night when you were being chased by them. Even worse, your consciousness may get wrapped in a confusing time-web. You would find it too difficult to get out of those webs. We don't have the luxury of time, my boy. As I taught you earlier think about only two things, anchor and destination. This is your anchor; this time, this world, this chamber. Focus only on this. Am I clear?"

Tej nodded his head in affirmation and laid motionless. Two of Rigu's disciples, Manika and Gajendra, entered the chamber. Manika was a girl in her late teens and had a pleasant smile on her face. Gajendra was the exact opposite, with a long, sturdy, well-muscled build. He had a grim, stony expression on his face. Both wore the ashram uniform of bright red and crimson white, like Rigu's own attire.

"Tej, meet two of my best disciples. On the right is Manika. Don't let her age belie your impression of her; she is a time-reading virtuoso. On the left is the muscle-man of our ashram, Gajendra. You might have heard the stories that he can run a hundred kilometers at a stretch without getting tired. But he is also a learned man. He knows a lot of ancient texts by heart."

Tej smiled at both of them. Manika responded to him with an even brighter smile and slightly lowered her head in respect. Gajendra only nodded his head a little as an acknowledgment, while his lips did a slight movement. It was difficult to tell if he'd smiled or not.

Manika handed Rigu a small plate of sandalwood paste which she'd brought along with her. The guru used three central fingers of his right hand and took some paste from the plate. He smeared it on Tej's forehead.

"The sandalwood will keep your brain calm and your thoughts focused, and will help ease your travel. In a few moments, I will show you the sketches of Rudrakshini which I produced yesterday night. Until then, relax and anchor yourself in the current space and time. Think of nothing else."

Rigu signaled for Gajendra to stay there and asked Manika to follow him outside. They both came outside. Rigu closed the door behind him and made sure he shut it tight. The red luminosity of an impending sunrise was already brightening the beautiful gardens of the ashram.

Manika was a little confused by what Rigu had said inside. "Gurudev, why did you tell Tej you made Rudrakshini's sketches? I did those sketches after my time-reading on her yesterday."

"Kid, you know that I'm old. I no longer can read time with certainty, which is why I seek help from smart disciples such as you. God has gifted you with sunset boon of time-reading, and you are still young. Your readings are sharper, and your visions are much less hazy than mine are. But Tej is embarking upon this righteous voyage on my word and my word alone. If I tell him that I am too weak even to read the temporal vibrations, will he have any confidence in me as his guru?"

"No, but lying to…"

"Are you going to question my morals, Manika? Especially at this crucial time?"

"No, Gurudev."

Manika realized that the guru was not his usual calm self today. For some reason, he was restless and agitated. She firmly believed that right ends didn't justify the wrong means, yet she kept quiet.

"Are all your questions answered, kid? Can I ask mine now? The important ones?"

"Yes, Gurudev."

"So, tell me, what do you have for me from yesterday night's time-reading?"

Manika shook her head in negation. "Nothing has changed, Gurudev."

"What do you mean, nothing has changed? We have thrown Tej in the mix. He is a time-demon. His actions should have started impacting the timeline. The future should be different now. Are you sure you are reading the right date, December 23rd, 2072?"

"Yes. Since you met Tej yesterday and brought him to our ashram, the number of possible futures has increased. I could see four thousand, two hundred, and eighty-nine futures two days ago. But today, I can see a little over fifty-three thousand possible futures. Tej's decisions combined with Kumbh's original choices have increased the permutations of future multifold."

Rigu got even more restless. "Manika, you are one of the strongest time-reader of the Bhavi group. You remind me of my old disciple Kuntala. You know that the number of futures has no impact on our cause. They are mere possibilities. We need to know if the dominant future has changed or not. Let's discuss that, please."

"That's what I am saying. I studied the whole four years of 2069 to 2072. I also put a special focus on December 23rd, 2072. The dominant future is exactly the same. No detail has changed."

"That is impossible. Tell me the details."

"Right now?"

"Yes, right now. The fate of humanity is at stake, kid. If Tej's involvement is not going to change the future, I need to make other arrangements. Kumbh has to be stopped at any cost. I need to see if I can send more time-warriors to the future. I was bullish on Tej, but after listening to you, I am having my doubts. So tell me each detail of the dominant future before I embark him on the time journey."

Manika felt weak in her gut. The apocalyptic future Rigu was asking her to describe was becoming her perennial nightmare. Rigu's insistence on her describing it, again and again, felt like a punishment. Rigu stretched his eyebrows as he looked at her as if waiting for her to begin anytime soon.

She took a deep breath as she began her narration. She covered the details around Concordia VX. Kumbh would enter the body of the hacker Karlesha. He would deploy the kill order for billions of souls. By the end of her narration, Manika burst into tears.

"What a fool this Kumbh is," Rigu murmured to himself. "He and his brother ruthlessly executed so many people in the past, and he has the exact same soul reaping plans for the future. The irony is that he will own this deadly world-ending power only because of artificial intelligence—a technology built by mankind for its benefit.

"Now, will you please stop crying, Manika? We have

a lot to do. We will need you to have another reading of this same vision after Tej begins his time travel today to Rudrakshini's time-slice. I hope that the dominant future will change after he does that."

"No, Gurudev, not anymore. I cannot live through this soul-crushing vision again and again."

Rigu wanted to scold her but realized he needed to take a softer approach. Use of strong words and reproach would not soothe her.

"Manika, when I first visited you three years ago, you were having those hazy visions of the future. You were only starting to realize your power as a time-reader, while I was ending my years-long journey. Look at how far you have come since, all from your decisive efforts to enhance yourself.

"From drawing those vague caricatures of time visions to being a powerful time-reader, your skill has grown in leaps and bounds. I want you to stay even more focused at this crucial moment. Time-reading can be a boon and a curse at the same time. Unfortunately, for you, it's the latter. Thicken your skin to sustain the mental trauma which comes with this power. Through our efforts, we can alter that horrifying future and save those innocent lives. If that is the case, don't you think your pain of living through it a few times is worth it?"

Manika nodded in affirmation as she wiped her tears. Composing herself, she continued, "Gurudev, does Tej know the details of this future?"

"No, he doesn't. He only knows that countless lives are in peril, and I don't even want to give him more details. The less he knows, the better, at this point in time. It may bias his actions and make our future predictions even more convoluted. So you should not mention a word of this to him. I will reveal specific details to him later as required. Let's go inside. Tej needs to play this visit with Rudrakshini, right? Otherwise, he will not even come back from where he is going."

They both went inside. The sun had now risen beyond the horizon, and its red rays were sneaking out from behind the shade of the ancient mountains.

8

THE SPELL OF REANIMATION

While Rigu and Manika were outside, Tej made several attempts to strike a conversation with Gajendra. It was all in vain. Even to his elaborate questions, he only got guttural sounds as a reply. When he tried to get up a couple of times, Gajendra stretched out his arm towards him and showed him his large palm, signaling him to stay where he was.

Fortunately for him, Rigu and Manika soon came back into the room. Tej noticed that Manika's face had a sullen look. She was not as cheerful as when she'd left a few minutes ago.

"What happened, Gurudev? Is everything all right?" Tej tried to sit but was again sternly signaled by Gajendra to not do so.

"All is fine Tej, don't worry. Manika please hand me over the sketches of Rudrakshini."

Manika handed him a bundle of sheets of paper, on which several elaborate charcoal sketches were drawn. Rigu went through the sketches and picked one. He returned the rest to Manika and showed the chosen sketch to Tej.

"Look at this, Tej and think of time, around three hundred and five years ago. I want you to go to a time five years before her death."

The sketch portrayed a lady with a heavy build, wearing a black dress and a necklace of skull and bones. She was looking towards the sky. Her arms were stretched out as if summoning some paranormal entity. In front of her lay the body of a frail man on a stone block.

"Oh, is she Rudrakshini? But who is this man lying in front of her, Gurudev?"

"I'll explain to you what's happening in this sketch because this is the exact moment you have to travel to. Rudrakshini is a master of dark sciences. In this sketch, she is performing her legendary re-animation ceremony, where she awakened the dead. The family members of this man brought this body in front of her. They want her to bring this body to life."

"Bring a dead body to life? That's magic, Gurudev."

"The parts of science you don't understand will always look like magic to you. But that does not mean it is magic. Rudrakshini had mastered a reanimation spell. She knew that human consciousness doesn't completely leave the body for thirteen days after death. That's the time it needs to let go of the vessel. With her reanimation spell, Rudrakshini could pull that departed consciousness into the body for one day before it left the body for another realm again."

"So a dead person gets to live, but only for one day?"

"Yes—sunrise to sunset, to be precise. Many people came to her with the cadaver of their loved one, and she cast the reanimation spell every day at sunrise. But she had three strict conditions. First, the death should not have happened more than one day prior. Second, the person should have died a natural death, as she couldn't revive damaged cadavers. And third, she promised to only reanimate the body only once. At dusk, the body drops dead again."

"Only from dawn to dusk? So people come to her to have their loved ones live for only one extra day?"

"Yes. What wouldn't you give to spend one more day with your mother, Tej? But what they don't realize is that they will lose their loved one at dusk again. It's like losing your beloved twice in such a quick span."

Tej felt empathy for the people who lost their loved ones. Who wouldn't want to spend time with their family member who was going far away, and forever? He remembered his mother's funeral ceremony for a moment, but quickly re-focused on the present. He did not want another stern reprimand from the guru.

Rigu continued. "So, if you focus on this sketch here, Rudrakshini is casting the reanimation spell to revive a middle-aged shepherd by the name Shambhu. Shambhu lived at a nearby village and died a day before this day. As she summons Shambhu's consciousness, the vessel is empty. You can enter the vessel riding through her reanimation spell. This spell will ease your movement into this body."

"And Shambhu's soul? Where will that go? Will I not be preventing his soul from entering his own body?"

"Don't worry about that, Tej. Our cause is far more important. Mankind will pay a very hefty price for Kumbh's actions in the future. Saving countless human lives is more important than an old shepherd reuniting with his family for one day."

"But Gurudev…"

"Do I need to repeat myself?"

"No, I have a different question," Tej said in a subtly rebuking tone but maintained a respectful stance. He, too, realized that Rigu was not his usual self today, but could not understand the reason why.

"Go on." Rigu was losing patience with Tej and his questions.

"My consciousness will travel to three hundred years in the past. Do they speak Sanskrit, as we do?"

"No, Tej, not exactly. They speak another dialect of Sanskrit called Vanibhransh."

"Then how will I communicate with them?"

Seeing that Rigu was getting impatient, Manika stepped in. "Gurudev, can I explain this? With your permission, please?" Rigu nodded and asked Gajendra to walk over to a corner with him, while Manika came near Tej.

"Manika, did I get your name right?" Tej asked. He was tired of seeing Gajendra's brick-stern face. Even Guru Rigu was on the edge. Among all this, Manika's beautiful eyes and her chirpy voice sounded welcoming to him.

"Yes, I'm Manika. Okay, let me explain it to you. As soon as your consciousness enters another body, it will have full access to all the body functions. You will also gain full control over the organs. So you will have access to the host's brain, his memory, his habits, tastes, likes, dislikes, and etcetera."

"So when I am inside of that person's head, I will become that person?"

"Yes. Getting into a brain may be overwhelming at first. For the first few seconds, you may sense a lot of new information coming to you, so relax your mind.

As regards to language, when the first word slips off your tongue, you will actually start to speak in the same language as your host does. At the same time, you will also comprehend what others near you are speaking. After a few moments, you will be exhibiting most of the natural behaviors the host used to exhibit. But at the inside, you will remember your anchor world and will have total control over the host. My advice would be, give it some time."

Rigu finished his conversation with Gajendra and came over to Tej. He touched his head softly and said, "I should apologize, Tej. I poured my anger out on you earlier. I am desperate to win this battle, to get rid of Kumbh and be of some service to mankind before I die."

"I understand, Gurudev. I'm ready to follow your instructions."

"I can't tell you what exactly will happen there. You will make your own decisions, which will keep altering our time visions. But remember two pieces of advice. First, don't accept the gift, and second, everybody has an ego."

"I don't quite understand what you said, Gurudev."

"Just repeat what I said."

"You said, don't accept the gift, and everybody has an ego."

"Again."

"Don't accept the gift, and everybody has an ego."

"Good. Engrave these two facts on the canvas of your mind. These will guide you when you make decisions there. This is your first time-voyage, son. As I told you earlier, you will have to recite the Trikaaldevi mantra seventy-nine times. Close your eyes. Have this sketch of

Rudrakshini performing re-animation spell on Shambhu etched into your mind. Concentrate on Shambhu's body and recite the mantra."

Tej closed his eyes and focused his mind on the mental picture he had formed of that sketch. He knew there were a lot of questions to which he wanted the answers, but some would come to him in due time. He first said his prayers to his mother, his guru, and started chanting the mantra of Goddess Trikaaldevi. He continuously thought of Shambhu's body and kept reciting the mantra. After repeating the mantra a few times, he felt a little cold, but nothing was happening.

I knew it would not work, he thought to himself. But he was afraid to open his eyes, as he feared the guru might scold him for not properly attempting it. He did a few more recitals, but after a few seconds, he got irritated, opened his eyes and sat up. "It's not working, Gurudev, I don't know why."

But his surroundings had completely changed. He was no longer in that chamber in Rigu's ashram. He was in Rudrakshini's reanimation chamber in the year 3362 BC. His first jump had been successful! He was three hundred and five years in the past.

9
RUDRAKSHINI, THE QUEEN OF NECROMANCERS

Tej realized he was sitting on the same ceremonial altar on which the body of Shambhu lay, as shown in the sketch. He looked around. On his left side, he saw Rudrakshini staring at him with wide eyes. Her left hand's index finger was pointed at him, while her right arm was stretched out in the air. Her right hand held a human skull smeared with a red powder. She was over eighty years old, but her sharp facial features and glaring eyes looked intimidating.

He attire was frightening, too. She had a long brown religious mark right in the middle of her forehead. Her long white hair, pitch black robe, and a large skull and bones necklace were making her appearance even more menacing.

Tej shifted his gaze away from her and looked around the room. Right near his feet, seven middle-aged women stood in a straight line formation. Each of them had their index fingers sandwiched between their tongue and lower teeth as if they were evocating some strange noise from their mouth. Each of them was dressed like Rudrakshini. On his right side stood at least a hundred villagers. Most had tears in their eyes, and their hands clasped in prayer. Some of them had big drums hanging around their necks, with strong sticks to beat them. But Tej realized a strange thing. They were all frozen.

Rudrakshini, those seven women, and the villagers were all stationary, like statues; as if a mysterious power had taken the whole chamber and the people in it, and turned them into a wax replica of themselves.

"Why are you all not moving, or saying anything?" Tej asked slowly in a low-pitched voice. His own voice sounded so different to him. He did not know what to make of this situation. Rigu or Manika hadn't told him what to do in this scenario. Would they remain frozen like this? Should he return to his own time? But how would he do that?

"Should I focus on my anchor and recite the mantra? Will I then travel back to my anchor?" He murmured to himself.

He heard a faint voice in his left ear. "Breathe." He turned left and again looked at Rudrakshini. He had a faint suspicion that she was saying the word "Breathe!" He noticed that although she was not moving at all, her eyeballs were showing motion. It was a frightening sight.

He gulped in fear and took a deep breath. As soon as he did that, the whole room got lively with a jolt, and everybody started moving. Tej had to clasp his ears because of the loud, screeching noises which struck his ears. Rudrakshini was chanting a mantra loudly. The seven women were rapidly moving their index fingers between their tongue and teeth, making a strange tribal noise. The villagers were whipping the drums, some of them even dancing to the tunes.

This clamor continued for a few moments before Rudrakshini shouted at top of her voice. "Quiet, everyone!" The whole room came to pin-drop silence.

"Shambhu? Are you back for good?" Rudrakshini demanded.

"I am not…" Tej was at loss for words. He looked again to the right to the crowd of villagers. He could recognize his wife, his mother, and two sons in the front row. They were looking at him with expectations as if waiting for him to say a few words.

But they were not his family. He looked at his wrinkled hands, his dress—they looked so alien. He caught up to the realization that he was inside another person's body.

A surge of memories swept through his brain. New people, new areas, and good and bad memories from the past were slowly coming to him. He was remembering vivid incidents from years ago.

But he knew he never experienced them before. They were not his memories. This is what Manika mentioned. Shambhu's reminiscences were coming to him in a huge tidal wave of information. Tej had difficulty breathing— he felt as if his throat was collapsing on the inside. He tilted back his head with a jerk, and his eyeballs started moving rapidly. His limbs got stiff. He was going into a seizure.

"Everyone out! Right now!" Rudrakshini thundered. Her voice echoed as if bouncing off the dark stone walls of the chamber. Her devotees started pushing people outside.

Rudrakshini took a small glass filled with a tranquilizer and held Shambhu's otherwise shaking jaw open tight.

She poured a few drops from it into Shambhu's mouth and kept the rest away. In a few moments, the whole room cleared. Shambhu was still lying on the ceremonial altar, wheezing. The tranquilizer had eased his fit. Rudrakshini paced through the room in anger, taking sharp steps back and forth. Her loud breathing indicated that she was fuming with anger.

"Water, please?" Tej asked in a feeble voice as he sat upon the altar. His face had a dead-tired look.

"Liar, deceiver! You are not Shambhu. His consciousness would not have rejected this body as yours did. He would not have fallen into a fit like this. Who are you? A ghoul, a lost consciousness, or some demon from hell?"

Rudrakshini brought her face so close to Shambhu's. Had she been any closer, their noses would have touched. "Speak, you devil, or be ready to face the wrath of Rudra!"

"I am a…", Tej was petrified to the core. He couldn't say even one word.

Rudrakshini dug her gaze into his own. "If you don't disclose your actual identity straightaway, I will condemn you to the worst of the hell fires for the rest of the eternity. Your consciousness will be a prisoner in the nethermost echelons of the inferno. There, a devil-priest will slice and dice you day after day, till the end of time!" Rudrakshini forewarned. For a moment, the whole of her chamber slightly shook and all the candles burning in there flickered.

Tej collected his courage. "I will tell you the truth. I am here to tell you the truth."

"You better do that!"

Tej narrated his whole story to Rudrakshini. He

started from his childhood, the encounter with Kumbh and Vetri. He also gave details on the last few days, how Rigu approached him, and how he'd traveled from three hundred and five years in the future to this date in the past.

Rudrakshini listened to him without saying a word. She realized he was not lying and offered him water. "Hmm. It's an interesting story, Tej. So you are a time-demon, ha?"

"I would say a time traveler, ma'am."

"Yeah, you time travelers are all the same to me, ha. I cannot understand why you do it. I understand paranormal realms; I understand Heaven and Hell. This time travel crap doesn't interest me. What do you want from me?"

"Guru Rigu said that you have a powerful spell which can help you control any consciousness. I want to learn that spell as your disciple."

Rudrakshini cachinnated, and her whole body shook. "You must be kidding, boy. There are people who've lived as my disciples for over fifteen years. I have not even taught them a single exorcism spell. Here you arrive today, riding your high horse, weaving stories of capturing some demon and helping mankind, etcetera. And you want me to help you right away? Listen, kid— be my disciple for two years, and then I will consider teaching you spells."

Tej went quiet.

"Although there is one thing I can do." Rudrakshini looked at Tej as if evaluating him. He felt hopeful.

"Since you came asking for help, I will not let you leave empty-handed. It would give me a bad name. I also feel a lot of wrongs have been done to you by God and nature. I sympathize with you. So I have an offer for you."

"An offer?"

"Yes. How would like to have a new life? An entirely new beginning?"

"A new life?" This conversation was not going where Tej wanted it to—towards the demon-invocation spell.

"Yes. A seven-year-old girl Tarika, who lived nearby, died yesterday evening. I am sure her consciousness has already left her body. Reanimation is challenging with small kids anyway. Their consciousness is not tied well enough to their meat and bones. Her parents are in a deep shock. But we can solve both their problem and yours. I can move your consciousness out of this frail old body of Shambhu the shepherd, and into that girl."

"What?"

"Yes, my boy. You can start over. Live your whole life again. Grow up, get loved, pampered, fall in love again, and get married. It's a fresh beginning, Tej. Take it."

This proposal baffled Tej. He felt Rigu somehow should have either time-traveled with him, or he should have prepared him better for this scenario. *What should he say now?*

"Come on, boy, what are you thinking? Would you not like that gift?"

Gift… that word echoed in Tej's mind. It instantly reminded him of the two pieces of advice Rigu had given right before his time jump. *'Don't accept the gift, and everybody has an ego.'*

"Don't accept the gift, and everybody has an ego," Tej murmured to himself.

"What was that? You said something?" Rudrakshini brought her ear near his mouth. "I am old, so I am hard of hearing. Can you please repeat yourself? Should I do the reanimation ritual on the kid with your consciousness?"

Tej thought on his feet. *Don't accept the gift. Yes, that's the right advice.* He would not accept this so-called gift. He had his own wife, daughter, and village to go back to. He was not going to spend the rest of his life in some girl's body. So that one part of the advice was fine.

But "everybody has an ego"—why did Rigu say that? Should he appeal to Rudrakshini's ego? Yes, that's how he would get her to co-operate. Rigu would have seen signs of her inflated ego in his time visions.

"I understand you need time to think. I will return by the afternoon. I want your decisive answer at that time." Rudrakshini turned and started to walk out of the chamber.

"You are the best," Tej whispered.

Rudrakshini stopped walking and turned back. "Can you be a little louder, kid? I can't hear you."

Tej got up from the altar and walked towards Rudrakshini. He got down on his knees and put his forehead on Rudrakshini's feet. Rudrakshini felt awkward.

He folded his hands in prayer and spoke in a humble tone. "O Rudrakshini Devi, the Queen of necromancers, please accept my salutations a thousand times over. You are the best necromancer this world ever had. No one like you ever existed, or will ever exist in this whole universe."

It was Rudrakshini's turn to stammer. "Yes, I mean, that's the truth. The whole world knows that. I'm the best." Sycophants around her praised her many times a day, yet she recognized a tone of pleading and humility in Tej's tone.

Tej went on, his hands folded and his gaze directed

towards Rudrakshini's feet. "My Guru told me to go after Kumbh because Kumbh is a peril for the survival of humanity. He wants to capture this demon for the benefit of others, for the whole of mankind. But Rudrakshini Devi, for me, this fight is personal. This demon and his brother kept me and my mother as slaves for years. They tortured us physically and mentally, threatened our lives day in and day out. They even outraged my mother's modesty." Tej's throat choked with emotions, and his eyes filled with tears. His anger towards Kumbh and his sharp desire for revenge had driven him to this point, and he had to use them.

Rudrakshini was silent. She had sympathy in her eyes.

"My mother is no longer alive, Rudrakshini Devi, but within you, I see another mother. A normal mother may give life to one or two children throughout her life. But you have given life to thousands of people by re-animating them. You are not only the best necromancer, but you are also the world's best mother. Please help me bring peace to the departed soul of my mother. She is no longer with me, and she cannot see me exacting my revenge from Kumbh. But if I am able to achieve that in my lifetime, I am sure I would be able to show my face to her in the afterlife. I beg you, as a son—please help me resolve the deepest conflict of my life. Please help me avenge her death."

"Shut up, kid." Rudrakshini's voice was heavy too.

"Please, Mother, if there's a price attached to your help, I will gladly pay it. Whatever it is," Tej begged again.

"I said, shut up. I will help you." Rudrakshini wiped a tear from her left eye and took a deep breath. "And stop crying like a baby. You got me all emotional, too."

Tej finally had a smile on his face, he wiped his tears.

"I will teach you the spell. But be aware that the demon-invocation spell comes with a death-condition."

"Death condition? What is that, Mother?"

"You will use this spell to achieve a goal, right?"

"Yes."

"If you use this spell, but fail to achieve that goal, then that counts as the failure of the spell, too."

"I don't understand?"

"Your goal is to entrap Kumbh in that body within the next six days, right?"

"Yes, a little less than six."

"So, if you use this spell, but cannot entrap Kumbh in that body by the sunset of the sixth day from now, you will fail, and the death-condition will apply."

"And what will happen then?"

"If you fail this aim, the spell would suck your consciousness from your body and throw it into an abyss. You can never return from that dark pit. If you accept this death-condition, only then can I teach you the spell."

Rigu had not mentioned anything like this—but Tej decided he would go with the flow.

"Mother, as I said, I will gladly pay any price. I accept. Please teach me."

"You are a valiant kid, son." Rudrakshini put her hand on Tej's head and blessed him. "I will now tell you a secret mantra. Recite it fifteen thousand times, I will be back in a while."

Rudrakshini brought her lips near to Tej's right ear and whispered a sacred chant into it.

"This chant? Fifteen thousand times? But I have to go back too, Mother."

"I know you are eager to go back. But, just because you are pressed for time doesn't mean the spell won't be learned the right way. This is the mantra of eternal Lord Shiva, destroyer of the universes. This chant is necessary before I can teach you the spell. Do you want to waste any more time by asking more inane questions? Or should I go and come back early so that I can help you?"

Tej folded his hands and bowed his head. Rudrakshini left the chamber, and Tej started his recital.

Rudrakshini returned after a few hours and found Tej waiting for her. She brought with her a small earthen pot which she showed to Tej. The pot was filled with a brittle green powder.

"Are you ready to learn, boy?" she asked.

"Yes. I'm ready."

"Fifteen thousand chants of the mantra have made sure you have assimilated the spell within you. It's a weapon waiting to be used. But there is a systematic way in which the weapon needs to be invoked.

"Whenever you want to invoke a demonic consciousness and control it, the first step is to establish a blood-connection. This connection is established with the host in which the demon resides. Blood is the second most important life force in the body, after the *praan-vaayu*, the life-giving-air you inhale. Blood flows throughout the body, most of it through the brain, constantly taking life to the brain and back to the organs. Hence, to control a consciousness which resides in the brain, you need a blood-connection first."

"How will I establish a blood-connection, Mother?"

"That is where this *bhasm*, this sacred powder, will help." Rudrakshini showed him the green powder again.

"First, smear this powder on the whole palm of your right hand. Which hand?"

"Right…right hand."

"Then you need to take a sharp knife and slice your palm, right in the middle, like this." Rudrakshini moved her left index finger across an imaginary line on her right palm to show Tej exactly where he needed to make the cut.

"Okay."

"Make sure the blood flows out of it and gets mixed with this powder. Do the same with the right hand of the host body, make sure his blood drips too."

"Okay."

"And while you are still chanting the mantra, clasp both the palms together, yours and his. The blood-connection will establish. After that, look into the vessel's eyes. Once you do that, you will have complete control over the demonic consciousness inside that vessel. That, in a true sense, is demon invocation and control."

"But I have one question if you don't mind?"

"Why would I mind? It's important that you ask as many questions as possible. This spell, although a simple one, is quite powerful. It should not go wrong."

"I understood the spell, but how will I take this powder with me? My consciousness will go to my body three hundred and five years in the future. But this powder—how will I take this with me?"

"You are an intelligent boy, but do you think you are smarter than I am?"

"No, I didn't mean that, Mother."

"Did you think you are the first time-demon who's come and asked me for help?"

"No, Mother."

"There is a simple way to transfer objects from the past to the future. There is a clan of priests who call themselves *vaahaks*, the carriers. Vaahaks keep objects safe and transfer them from generation to generation. They only give it to a specific individual in the future, who comes to them on a specified day, with a specified code-word. The best part is that they are very secretive. Books, letters, artifacts, any objects of small size are safe with them.

"I will give this powder to the high-priest of a temple nearby who is a vaahak. He and his clan will make sure they and their sons and their grandsons keep it safe until a traveler to the future collects this from them. I will also give them a code-word. They will only hand it over to the person who says that code-word."

"Okay. Where is this temple, and what is that code-word, Mother?"

"I won't tell you that."

"But how will I find it in future?"

"You ask too many questions, boy. Your guru is a time-reader, right? Ask him to check his visions of this time-slice. After this visit of yours, the visions will update themselves. He will have his answers. Now, don't waste more of my time, or I'll change my mind. Go back the same way you came."

"I can't thank you enough, Mother, and …"

"Go now!"

Tej touched Rudrakshini's feet and again placed himself on the altar table. He closed his eyes and recited the time travel mantra given by his Guru. But this time, he was far more comfortable and relaxed. He felt he did not even need the mantra. He only needed to concentrate on his own body lying on the altar in Rigu's ashram, his anchor. It was time to return to the source.

10
KAAL-VAAHINI, THE RIVER OF TIME

This time jump was different for Tej. At first, he felt he was being thrown across a huge, shining tube of light. But then he saw a spectacle which jolted his senses. He was flying towards a gigantic astronomical body, a pitch-black abyss, the periphery of which was gleaming with bright light. It was a supermassive black hole, sucking him in at lightning speed. As he was drawn near, he had to clench his eyes due to the dazzling sharpness of the peripheral glow.

But when he opened his eyes, he was in an unexpected place. While he'd expected that he would land in his original body, he was sitting in a boat floating through a river. The waters were murky and silent. The sky was overcast with dense clouds, and the surroundings were full of mist.

"I must be dreaming. What is this place?" he murmured to himself. As the mist around his eyes cleared, he noticed that his friend Manu Kumar was sitting on the other end of the boat. Manu was sitting in a meditative pose, with his eyes closed.

"Manu, what are you doing here? Where are we?"

Manu opened his eyes and looked at Tej as if he was seeing him for the first time in his life. He got restless and said, "What are you doing here, Tej? Jump in the water."

"Why, Manu? What is this?"

"I am not Manu. This is the *Kaal-vaahini*, the river of time. Jump in the water, or you will miss the exact moment you have to go to. You will be forever lost in endless tunnels of time. Jump right now!"

Tej jumped into the river and dove deep. The water started to fill his eyes, ears, and nostrils, and he gasped for air. He wanted to scream but the feeling of drowning was slowly suffocating the life from him. He pushed strongly towards the surface but went unconscious.

Chamber of Time-Travel, Rigu's Ashram
Year 3057 B.C.

"Tej, wake up, please. Can you hear my voice?" He could hear Manika calling out his name from a distance. He felt pressure on his right arm and woke up, panting. He was back on his anchor pod in Rigu's ashram. His whole body was perspiring. Manika was standing next to him, with an expression of concern on her face.

"What happened, Manika, what time it is? Has a lot of time passed? Where is Gurudev?"

"No, Tej, we are still on the second day. Don't worry," Manika assured him, and handed him a glass of water. "Where did you drift to, Tej? We expected that you would return two hours ago, but you were gone. I was getting worried." She poured him more water and he guzzled the whole glass as if he had been thirsty for ages.

"I don't know where I was. But how did you know I was supposed to return two hours ago?" Tej had a hard time thinking. His whole body felt stiff, and he had a severe headache.

"Our visions got updated; we saw your entire discussion with Rudrakshini. You did a good job of convincing her. Appealing to her ego and to her maternal side was a masterstroke. After that, we saw you starting your travel from there. I saw you entering the black hole, and you should've come out right away. But after that, you were un-locatable on the entire time horizon. Did you get confused about the exact location of your anchor?"

"No, I was clear that this was my anchor. But I don't know where I drifted to. Is it possible that I experienced a series of nightmares? At first, I was traveling toward a black sun. It was unlike anything I had ever seen. Then I was on a boat. Then I was drowning. I would need to ask Guru Rigu what all these dreams mean. Where is he?"

"Gurudev waited for some time for you to return. When you did not, he took a few disciples and went to the ancient temple where Rudrakshini preserved the sacred powder three hundred years ago. The old township where Rudrakshini used to practice necromancy is seventy-five kilometers from here. Even with the fastest horses, they won't return before the wee hours."

"But why did Gurudev have to go? He could have sent another disciple. We have so little time, we could have prepared for my travel to the future." Tej was feeling restless. He wanted all this to be over.

Manika smiled. "Why are you so restless, Tej? We won a small battle. You secured the demon invocation spell from Rudrakshini. Another step forward, towards your victory in this holy battle. Gurudev went himself because he didn't want to take any risks."

"What risks?"

"After reading your conversation with Rudrakshini, we also read a vision from the day after. That day, Rudrakshini handed over the sacred powder and the code-word to the head priest of the temple. We listened to the code-word, but Gurudev did not share it with anyone, not even Gajendra. Gurudev suspects that Kumbh may also be planning to stop us from capturing him. Hence, he is being cautious."

Tej looked at the bodies of time-demons at his sides and felt helpless. He so wanted to take a sharp sword and slash their necks, but he now understood those bodies were only vessels. For the time-demons, the only equivalent of death was perennial entrapment in one vessel.

He turned to Manika and looked into her eyes. "Manika."

"Yes?"

"You too are a time-reader, like Guru Rigu is. Isn't that right?"

"Yes, I am. He has been time-visioning for decades. But I am fairly new to this art."

"Can I ask you a question? I won't be able to ask this question of Gurudev."

Manika felt a little uncomfortable. What if Tej asked about the future? Rigu cautioned her against discussing the future with Tej. There was so much she knew from her visions and wanted to tell Tej, but doing so would be against the guru's strict orders. It would be a tough dilemma for her to handle.

"Tej, you look exhausted. Why don't you rest?" she deflected.

"No, I want to know the answer to this. This question is eating me from the inside."

Manika was tight-lipped.

"Manika, am I a time-demon too?"

"What?"

"Am I an evil presence in this world, like Kumbh and Vetri are? I have no intentions of hurting other people. But when I was talking to Rudrakshini, she referred to me as a time-demon. Although Gurudev told me earlier that I am a time-demon, the way she said it was different. Her tone implied a rather negative connotation. Am I another member of this demonic ilk? Will I become like them?"

Manika felt relieved—Tej was not asking about the future. She felt a strong feeling of sympathy for him. He was fighting for a righteous cause, putting his family, his life, and his whole being on the line—yet he was so pure of heart that he doubted his own intentions.

She sat near him. "Tej, since we both are disciples to the same Guru, you are like a brother to me. So please believe every word I am going to say."

Tej nodded.

"If you are a person with religious inclinations, you may view time travel as a boon from the Gods. If you have a scientific bent of mind, you may accept the fact that the ability to time travel is the next step in our evolution. After thousands of years of living within bodies made of bones and flesh, the consciousness evolved into living without them or searched for better bodies to be in. You can believe in either of these schools of thought. But either way, 'time-travel' is another power. Isn't it?"

"Yes, it is." Tej understood where she was going, but kept listening.

"So, like any other power, or any other weapon time-travel can be used for the betterment of mankind or for the destruction of it. A sword which kills can also be used to protect. There have been time travelers who have been messiahs, rabbis, philanthropists, leaders, and kings—people who did so much good again and again through their re-incarnations. They never went into the past with the aim of gaining power. Rather, they used the wisdom gained from previous births to spread positivity throughout the world.

"On the flip side, though, we have time travelers such as these two evil brothers, who derived strange mirth out of taking innocent lives. They lusted after money, power, and sexual pleasures. They are the demons of time in the truest diabolical sense. So as a time traveler who has actualized his power, you have a simple choice to make. Which side do you want to be on?"

"I understand, sister. Those were wise words. You have resolved a pang of strong guilt within me, which would have devoured me from within." Finally, after what felt like a long time, Tej smiled.

"Now, no more talk; you need to rest. Also, this cement block is uncomfortable—you need not lie on this till your next time jump. We have arranged a bed for you there." Manika signaled over to a cot which had been placed in the room, with a comfortable bed laid on to it.

"Take rest. I'll arrange food for you. When Gurudev returns, he will meet you."

Tej still felt stiff. Manika helped him walk over to the

cot and made him sit on it.

"Can I go outside, sister? I am suffocating in here."

"No, we have strict orders from Gurudev. You need to stay in this chamber. Your next time jump is near. We don't want you to disrupt this well-established anchor."

At this moment, Gajendra entered the room and marched towards Kumbh's body. Tej said hello to him, but as usual, received a guttural "Hmm" noise from him.

"Does he ever speak?" Tej whispered to Manika.

She let out a loud chuckle and whispered, "He does at times."

Gajendra picked a small metal pot filled with a dark liquid and dropped a few drops in both Kumbh and Vetri's mouths. He stood there for a moment, then trudged out of the room without saying a word.

"What did he just do?" Tej was surprised.

"He has to administer a medicinal dose to Kumbh. and Vetri's bodies daily. This dose has basic life-support nutrients and tranquilizers. Gajendra and other disciples have been doing this every day for the past twenty years without fail since Rigu captured these demons."

"Oh, so if this vessel stays in a state of sleep, Kumbh cannot escape it, even if he comes back?"

"No—if Kumbh ever returns to this vessel, we won't be able to stop him. Not even with these tranquilizers. He will unquestionably wake up, despite these medications administered to him. But one impact these medicines will have is that he will wake up delirious. In that state, he can again be manipulated to go to a Kaalshoonya, like the previous time Gurudev trapped him in Virtexo."

"Oh, so that's why he's kept on tranquilizers. And Vetri? Gurudev said he is forever entrapped in this body. Does he get the same dose?"

"Yes. But for him, this dosage only works as life support, so that the vessel does not die and Vetri stays trapped."

"One day, I want to learn this science stuff from you, sister. If I ask too many questions of Gurudev, I am afraid he will beat me with a stick."

Manika laughed again. "Okay, no more chit-chat. Lie down and take rest."

She left the room and locked it from the outside. Tej looked at the bodies of time-demons one more time, lay back, and closed his eyes. He was so tired that he slipped into the lap of sleep within a few seconds.

The next morning, when he opened his eyes, he saw a huge man standing next to him and got startled. It was Gajendra. He only stood there with his stone-faced expression and his hands behind his back.

"You were waiting for me to wake up, weren't you? And what are you holding in your hands, a dagger?" Tej joked. As usual, he got no reply. Tej got up, yawned, and stretched his hands.

"Gajendra, brother, I am planning to freshen up first. But where can I find a hot breakfast and some juicy fruit? I am especially looking forward to eating the fresh apples from those trees on the periphery of the ashram. They looked yummy."

"Get ready. Gurudev will come and meet you here," Gajendra said in a heavy, nonchalant tone, and walked outside.

"Wow, those were your first words to me, brother. And let me tell you, that's a good start to our friendship."

Before Tej could finish the sentence, Gajendra was out of the door.

Later, Manika brought some eatables, towels, and fresh clothes for Tej. She told him she'd brought food for him last night as well, but he was fast asleep, so she didn't wake him up.

Tej got ready and sat for breakfast. After he finished his meal, he got up but felt giddy. He quickly sat on the cot nearby. He felt a strange feeling of uneasiness for a few moments and took some time to shake it off. An hour later, Rigu entered the room and clutched Tej in a tight hug.

"Oh Gurudev, you are here." Tej was feeling awkward in the hug, but the guru didn't let go for a few seconds.

"Tej, my son, you did a great job yesterday. We have got Rudrakshini's sacred bhasm powder. I have made further arrangements for you to get the same powder in the future."

"In the same way as you got it from the past, Gurudev?"

"Similar, but not the same. This time, this powder has to stay safe for five thousand years, not a mere three hundred. I have chosen an ancient sect of vaahaks. They are priests who, I know from my time vision, adhere intensely to their customs and rituals. These vaahaks will inherit this sealed packet of sacred powder as an artifact in their ancient temple. When you travel to the future, you will have to go to them and retrieve it. I will transfer this powder into a puzzle box."

"A puzzle box?" Tej had never seen a puzzle box.

"Yes, it's a special box. The lid of this box will be encrypted with certain levers and buttons. These need to be pressed in a certain specific combination, and only then can the box be opened."

"So that no one other than me can open this box?"

"Yes."

"Okay, Gurudev. I wanted to ask—I also felt a little uneasy a few moments ago. I am not sure why."

"The reason for that, Tej, is that your consciousness is not fully back into this body. Remnants of it are still traveling through time, coming to you slowly. That is the exact phenomena which will ease your travel to the future. By sending you into the past, I have served another purpose. You will be able to slingshot into the future."

Rigu explained Tej the concept of a slingshot in time-travel. A stone placed in a slingshot is first pulled backward and then launched forward with a steep velocity. Using the same principle, by going into the recent past, Tej had pulled his consciousness further in the past. Now he would be thrown towards the future at a fast speed.

"I am sure I'll need a lifetime to understand these concepts, Gurudev."

"You are a time-demon, Tej, but one with righteous intentions. You will have not one but many lifetimes to learn. You may have been born human, but your consciousness is immortal. Get ready—you have a plane to catch."

"A plane?"

"Yes, a plane to catch and a cardiac arrest to survive through."

Day 3 of 7

11
FLIGHT VQ7101, DALLAS TO MUMBAI

It was almost afternoon when Tej and Rigu spoke about various subjects related to time travel. Tej's jump to the future was two hours away. While Tej was asking questions, Rigu held back his answers. He only mentioned those details which he felt Tej would absolutely need to succeed on his mission.

Tej was still wrapping his head around the concept of a slingshot in time travel. He was talking to Rigu, trying to understand what he meant by plane and a cardiac arrest when Manika entered the room.

She had bought piping-hot herbal tea for Rigu and Tej, along with some fresh fruit. She also brought sketches of the future date and time which represented Tej's destination. But Rigu didn't allow Tej to see them yet. He maintained that it would be better if Tej only saw the sketch at the exact moment when he needs to time-jump.

As he sipped that refreshing tea, Tej asked Rigu, "Why could I not have gone to the future yesterday itself, or a year earlier? That would have given me a lot of time to prepare."

Rigu explained to him that the flow of time is like a laminar flow of concrete. Time's course rarely changes, not unless time-demons return to the past and alter the course of events. Since Kumbh had already taken a body in the year 2024, they would have to be cautious of the time to which they sent Tej. If they sent Tej to, say, the year 2023 in the same location, it would affect Kumbh's actions in a way they don't know. When Kumbh possessed a body in 2024, Tej would already be present there. If that happened, Kumbh would sense the presence of another time-demon in the same location. Their actions would start impacting Kumbh's actions.

Time-readers usually tied together specific start and end points in two time-slices, essential for them to keep accurate track of impending events. Rigu and Manika tied the sunrise of the first day in 2024 AD, when the Kumbh escaped, with the sunrise of the day in 3057 BC, when Rigu came to visit Tej. Since then, they had been charting out the visions in both the time-slices hour by hour, in parallel. They had been updating their visions and taking further actions as needed.

Unable to understand much of these concepts, Tej decided it was best to keep quiet. No point asking questions for which the answers were beyond his comprehension.

Rigu also told Tej they could not identify Kumbh's specific host in the year 2024 yet, but they had triangulated Kumbh's location with reasonable accuracy. They knew that Kumbh has acquired a host somewhere in a city called Mumbai, in the India of the future.

"But you time-readers can read the exact future, Gurudev. You can find out where Kumbh went and which specific host he took with ease. Isn't that correct?"

"It's not that easy, Tej. Kumbh is an ancient time-demon. He knows that we time-readers will track his movements, and he knows how to cover his tracks. Whenever he takes a new body, he undertakes an action called a 'knock-off blitz' to throw us off his scent."

"A knock-off blitz?"

"Yes. As soon as he leaves his previous host, he zips through several hundred, even thousands of human brains. He takes up one of these bodies as a host. For rest, he knocks off their consciousness. It's nearly impossible for us time-readers to keep tracking him during this quick blitz, and we lose track. Even with a hundred time-readers, it can take us months to study these time visions. Only after a careful study, documentation, and tying them, can we deduce the exact host."

"And the people whose consciousness he represses, do they die?"

"Not necessarily. The people he knocks off feel a sense of dizziness. This happens because their consciousness is repressed for a few microseconds. Some of them faint; others only feel dizzy. Frail ones may actually die too."

"So from your visions, you know that Kumbh undertook this knock-off blitz after he escaped this time?"

"Yes, he did that two days ago when he escaped. Several thousand people throughout this city of Mumbai felt a sense of vertigo and a feeling of dizziness in the wee hours of the morning. Some of them were in deep sleep at that time so they did not feel it. But great numbers of those who were awake reported it the next day. Investigative authorities couldn't identify why so many people felt dizzy around the same time. This incident got attributed it to some kind of gas leak controversy theory. But we know it was Kumbh's doing."

Tej grasped the greater part and understood that he had to go to a place called Mumbai five thousand years in the future to find where Kumbh was.

Rigu gave Tej some papers to read, bearing a description of the host Tej was to acquire in the future. After looking at several options, Rigu's team had selected a specific individual in Mumbai who was best suited for Tej. His name was Ravi Kumar Cheri. He was an international illegal arms dealer in the guise of a successful businessman.

The rationale behind choosing that host was that Tej should get a host who was influential. Kumbh too would have most likely possessed a host with money, business contacts, and political relations. The time of Tej's transit had also had been chosen with care. He would be able to enter his host at his weakest moment: his death.

"So when I take his host body, Gurudev, I would repress this Ravi Kumar's original consciousness, as time-demons do?"

"No, Tej, we will not act like those demons. We don't want you to possess a live body. We will do the same exercise as we did with Shambhu, your previous host. Ravi is going to die in a few minutes. You will enter his body a few seconds after his death, soon after his consciousness leaves his body—but before his brain dies due to lack of oxygen. A brain-dead body is a worthless host."

Tej was making some sense of what was going to happen. He closed his eyes and relaxed.

Business Class Cabin, Onboard Flight VQ7101

At the same moment in the year 2024 AD, Ravi Kumar Cheri was sitting on his comfortable business class seat onboard VJM-Pacific Flight VQ7101. This was the longest flight from Dallas to Mumbai. The airliner was cruising at eleven thousand feet and had crossed the North Pole.

Ravi was a smart-looking man in his mid-thirties, with a healthy build, wide face, and a thick mustache. He wore a light blue formal shirt and black trousers. He had a golden pen in his left shirt pocket and wore a shining Ulysse Nardin watch on his left wrist. He was sipping a premium scotch, eating roasted cashews, and watching a live Euro Cup football match between Germany and Turkey. He was also sending WhatsApp messages to several ladies in his "friends" group in Mumbai.

The flight was only a hundred minutes out from its destination when Ravi felt a slight uneasiness in his chest. He was also feeling shortness of breath. He attributed it to too much scotch and the constant turbulence the plane dealt with while crossing over the North Pole.

"Are you okay, Mr. Cheri?" asked Pamela, an air hostess who was passing by the aisle. She noticed that Ravi had a hand on his chest. Ravi had been flirting with her a couple of hours ago when he went to fetch a drink at the bar, so he was the last person she wanted to talk to. Still, on seeing him uncomfortable, she felt concerned.

"Yeah…yeah, Pamela, yes. I had too much to drink. Can I get some hot black coffee? That may bring me to my senses." Ravi still felt an uneasiness in his chest and stiffness in his neck.

"Coming your way right away, sir." Pamela gave him

a wide, plastic smile and went away, cursing under her breath.

"Isn't she a piece of melted butter?" Ravi exclaimed as he watched her walk away.

"Sorry?" A British passenger seated next to him and listening to music removed his large headphones. "You said something, sir?"

"No, no, I didn't. Please go back to your music." Ravi made a fake, smiling gesture.

Back in 3057 BC, Tej was seated again on the cement block, his physical anchor pod. Rigu and Manika were standing next to him. The moment of his time-travel was near.

From her visions, Manika knew that Ravi's enemies had poisoned him with a specific undetectable chemical designed to send his heart into an irregular rhythm, which would eventually cause a heart attack. After doing its job, the chemical would leave his body via sweat and urine within a few minutes. But the chemical had not reacted yet. In a few minutes, Ravi would experience a heart attack from which he would not recover, after which his consciousness would leave his body. It would be the ideal time for Tej to take his new host.

Manika told Tej that as soon as he acquired Ravi's body, he should pass urine, and the poison would exit his body. It would pose no further mortal danger to his vessel.

"The future is different, Tej. But don't worry. Like the last time, the host's memories, thoughts, habits, friends, and foes, will all be at your fingertips. Don't get overwhelmed. Give it some time," Manika said with a smile.

She knew the task that lay ahead was much more difficult and complicated. For a village boy, Tej, whose exposure to technology was no more advanced than his bow and arrow, to go into the year 2024 AD and succeed would be immensely difficult. For a decisive victory, he would have to assimilate the new technologies, gel into the environment, and understand the resources available to his host. On the other hand, his nemesis Kumbh was a primordial demon of time and a habitual time traveler. He had been to the future many times and was much more accustomed to it than Tej could ever be. The odds were low. But Tej had pulled off no less of a miracle by going to Rudrakshini and winning her trust. There was a flicker of hope that Tej would emerge a victor. But only "time" would tell.

Rigu looked at Tej as if he might never meet him again. "Tej, it's time for you to rote-memorize what the code-phrase is. You need to go to the ancient temple of Lord Shiva in a village called Bhramatipura near Mumbai. The code-phrase is a verse from *Shiv Mahapuraan*, one of the ancient Hindu Scriptures."

Rigu handed over a dried leaf with Sanskrit verse written on it to Tej. He recited it a few times, and then repeated it from memory.

"No advice for me this time, Gurudev?"

"Two pieces of advice again. First, Kumbh is a liar. You will meet him face to face. When you do, he will say anything to dissuade you from your aim. Just stick to your path, and you will taste the ripe fruit of success."

"And the second advice?"

"Be cognizant of the time. You have to get him before

the sunset of the seventh day."

"But why sunset, Gurudev? He got off at sunrise our time. Seven days means the sunrise of the eighth day. Isn't that right?"

"No, Tej. It's not exactly seven days—the seventh day is critical. He is an old time-demon; he can establish his anchor anytime on the seventh day. My experience is that the sunset of the seventh day is a strong cut-off. The sun is a heavenly body which interferes with time-travel. His anchor would be finally established on the seventh day itself. As soon as the sun sets on his geo-locale on the seventh day, he will bolt out of 2024 and go into the farthest future, where he has plans to take billions of lives."

"Billions?"

"Yes—it's inconceivable, unthinkable, but it's true. The stakes are high, Tej, and a lot is riding on you. And I won't mince my words—the task before you is daunting. But you have the element of surprise. He doesn't know who is coming for him and how we plan to capture him. Keep your eyes on the clock."

"Sunset of the seventh day. I will remember Gurudev."

Rigu again applied sandalwood paste on Tej's forehead. "It's time, my son. May victory be yours."

Tej closed his eyes and started chanting the mantra of the time-goddess. He focused on the sketch which Rigu showed him, in which Ravi was unconscious because of cardiac arrest. The flight cabin crew was struggling to re-start his heart using a defibrillator. That was his time-slice destination.

Ravi had opened the top two buttons of his shirt, feeling as if a heavy stone was placed on his heart. He was sweating a lot when he called for the cabin attendant. He also asked the air-hostesses to inform two of his co-passengers in economy class. His co-passengers were actually his bodyguards, who usually traveled with him in plain-clothes. What he did not realize was that the plan to murder him was already set in motion. There was nothing those two bodyguards could do.

Ravi laid back on the chair and tried to relax, but his body was giving up. His heart's ventricular fibrillation was getting severe. He felt a sudden shooting pain, after which he suffered a cardiac arrest and went unconscious.

One of the cabin attendants checked his pulse and knew what she had to do. The crew was trained in using a defibrillator. They brought the apparatus and tried to resuscitate him a few times, but the pulse was gone. The bodyguards came running, but they stood by, helpless. This was not a threat they could protect their boss against.

The co-passengers looked on with absolute shock as a man died right in front of their eyes. An old lady started sobbing as the pale, lifeless body of Ravi Kumar Cheri lay stiff on the plane seat. One of the air-hostesses went to inform the pilot that one of the passengers was deceased. Another one started to make a sad broadcast on her announcement system.

But Ravi suddenly sprang back to life with a deep breath. His pupils were widened, his face was mottled a little, and he was gasping for air as if he had just been smothered.

Those who saw him coming back expressed sighs of shock, and some even clapped. Two air-hostesses hugged each other. Few passengers nearby chanted their deities' names. They had witnessed a miracle. A guy who'd died a few moments ago rebounded from jaws of death. Little did they know he was no longer Ravi Kumar Cheri—he was Tej.

12
EARS AND EYES OF AN INTERNATIONAL GANGSTER

ej recollected himself and let the muscle memory of his host guide him. He ordered the bodyguards to return to their seats, though they insisted on standing near him for the rest of the journey. He felt too weak to walk, but as instructed by Manika, he had to go and pass urine. He spent the rest of his flight journey with his eyes closed and rarely spoke to others.

A flood of Ravi's memories streamed into his consciousness, but this time, he was calm. He didn't let the host memories overwhelm him, as they had with Shambhu.

He started reading Ravi Kumar Cheri's whole life like a textbook, from his hazy childhood to the present day. Ravi's journey had taken him from childhood as a poor farmer's kid in a small village in Tamil Nadu, India to a global illegal arms dealer, an international criminal who operated under the radar of the world's best law enforcement agencies. Good, bad, sweet, bitter memories. His achievements in business, his loss of loved ones, his ventures into the dark side, his first foray into the land of illegal arms dealing. His friends, political connections, safe-houses, foreign bank accounts, illegal business dealings. His known associates, his strong competitors, his arch-enemies. All these details were as clear and manifest in Tej's mind as if they were his own memories.

Ravi had started as a normal government contractor around seventeen years ago. Over time, he built his clout among bureaucratic and political circles. Within a few months, the line between what was legal and what was not, blurred out for him. He has been dealing with small and big guns and bombs for the past fifteen years. Recently, he'd started dealing in chemical weapons such as mustard gas, hydrogen cyanide, and Sarin. These new deals made him an even more potent death merchant.

His parents lived in an old village, which he rarely visited. His only sibling was an elder sister, whom he had not seen or talked to in a few years. He had married once, got divorced, and had no children. His only love interests were his ever-changing mistresses. The latest one was Tanisha Mahadevan, a young, upcoming actress from Southern India's film industry. Rujeeth Kumar and Abbas Shafi were two of his closest business associates. Naahan was his personal bodyguard and driver in India. He would receive Ravi at the Chhatrapati Shivaji Maharaj International Airport in Mumbai.

Although these memories did not trouble Tej, he was overwhelmed by the technology. High-tech advancements of this distant future were convoluted riddles to him. Phones, laptops, computers, and TV screens were strange artifacts, which he had a tough time comprehending. These gadgets fascinated as well as intimidated him. Last but not least, the fact that he was sitting in a huge carriage weighing millions of kilograms baffled him. Heaped upon that, this prodigious machine was somehow flying through the air, carrying hundreds of passengers. This was a miracle to him. His ability to travel through time, though miraculous, had a supernatural feel to it. But all this technology? It was built by humans and was close to unbelievable.

What was most annoying to him so far was that he felt the need to check his phone again and again. He scrolled through his messages, emails, and stared at the phone screen. Long-term habits had encoded these activities into Ravi's muscle memory. Tej let that muscle memory take over these mundane tasks. Ravi's brain knew how to deal with these regular situations best, and Tej followed those instincts.

Upon landing, Tej went through the usual Customs and Immigration. He relied on Ravi's brain to sleepwalk through galleries, queues, smiles, and handshakes, even producing relevant documentation. At Customs, though, he felt his heartbeat rising for no reason. He realized that Ravi was uneasy while going through it. But it all went smoothly.

While waiting for his baggage at belt number five, Tej saw a tall, handsome man standing at the adjoining conveyer belt. He wore a dark green three-piece suit with a dark orange designer tie. He also had a golden brooch on his coat pocket.

Tej found the man very well-dressed and charming. His facial features were appealing, too. He had beautiful eyes, well-done eyebrows, a thin, slanting nose, and a broad jaw. His clean-shaven face gleamed under the bright ceiling lights. Tej had rarely seen a more gorgeous man.

If Manu Kumar lived in this age, he would have dressed exactly like this. Tej thought and smiled to himself. He thought of exchanging numbers with Mr. Handsome but decided against it. He kept stealing glances until the man's suitcase arrived, and he left.

After collecting his bags, Tej walked towards the exit, where his attentive, loyal, and careful employee Naahan received him. Naahan escorted him to his BMW V9 Coupe.

A kilometer outside the airport, two armed gunmen also joined them in the car. Another car full of five armed personnel also followed them for the rest of their journey. On usual occasions, Ravi traveled light, with only Naahan as his company. It was important for him to maintain the façade that he was actually a normal businessman, but given the recent attempt on his life, Naahan felt these precautions were mandatory.

Armed with the knowledge of Ravi's brain, Tej got lost in introspection throughout the way. Amidst the vagaries of this futuristic new world, assiduous thoughts of capturing Kumbh lurked at the back of his mind. He needed Ravi's resources, and he needed to mobilize them fast to hunt for Kumbh. He knew that there was a team of private detectives on Ravi's payroll who could do this with ease, but he needed to take his close associates Rujeeth and Shafi into his confidence. It was important before he took any further steps. There was no question of revealing his identity and his true aim to them, so he would have to devise a story which would work for this world and this time.

He recalled that in Dallas, Ravi had attended several meetings with a machine tools company called Rock & Apostle Inc. But the machine tools were a false front for a money-laundering firm which Ravi used on regular basis. These details sparked his imagination, and a plan took shape in his mind.

Tej was witnessing another time-demon gift. Ravi's brain was working to fulfill Tej's desires without explicit instructions from Tej. The brain had realized that the eventual aim was to capture Kumbh, and it was devising strategies to reach that aim.

Tej didn't delve into the "why" and "how" of these strategies. He went with the flow in the direction Ravi's brain was taking him. He had to reach Kumbh and exact his revenge. That burning desire drove him forward.

He asked Naahan to not take his car to his mansion at Nariman Point. Instead, he ordered him to drive to a reticent bungalow on the outskirts of the city. Ravi's brain suggested that this could be the best place for him to stay away from the bustling noises of the city, and act upon his plan in peace. Tej also messaged for Rujeeth and Shafi to meet him at the bungalow as soon as possible.

As the car rolled through the giant gates of Ravi's bungalow, Tej was awed by the beauty of that mesmerizing property. The bungalow had lush green gardens and beautiful red-brick pathways. Multicolored flower beds and a music-synced fountain apparatus further added to its beauty. On the inside, imported tiling work and antique pieces bedecked its huge walls. There were minimal servants in the bungalow, but there were dozens of armed men both inside and outside the premises, watching over the place twenty-four-seven.

A huge Lord Ganesh statue stood at the entrance of the main bungalow building. A mere look at that statue got Tej emotional. Lord Ganesh was the deity at his temple in his village, too. He stopped for a moment and said a quick silent prayer to the Lord. At last, he saw some semblance of his past in this otherwise strange future.

Once inside, he had a temptation to take a long, hot shower. Ravi enjoyed it, too.

While bathing, he noticed that Ravi's body had quite a lot of scars—bullet and knife wounds. His enemies had shot as well as stabbed him a few times. Those were Ravi's traumatic memories and dark areas of his past, through which Tej did not want to venture.

He stepped out and changed into fresh clothing. Tanisha was sending him WhatsApp messages. She was on a trip to Bhutan with her girl gang and was missing him. She promised to fall into his arms next week. Tej smiled as he read those words, though he didn't know why he did so. He remembered Manu Kumar.

After getting ready, he came to the dining area and got seated. He knew it would take time to get used to the cuisines of this age. He was not yet ready to put a food item called a "tuna sandwich" inside his mouth. He only ate bananas and apples, drank some cold water, and sat waiting for Rujeeth and Shafi.

When they arrived, the three of them sat outside in the garden for drinks, lounging on comfortable chairs. The red sun skimmed the horizon, and the day was coming to an end. They started to chat.

"Who could have poisoned you, boss?" Shafi asked, relishing his premium vodka.

"We'll get to that later. None of you asked me how my meeting with Rock & Apostle went." Tej eyed both his associates.

"Okay…yes, how did it go?" Rujeeth sounded nervous.

Tej knew that both men were quite high up in his organization, but he was their boss.

"Not well. I met Joshua Barkell, their head of accounts," Tej said in a grim tone.

"Yup, I know that chap. Brilliant guy. Harvard educated. Knows economics and international trade laws by heart. A sharp asset for them," Rujeeth quipped.

"But too sharp for us, too. He wants us to raise their service fee by 0.25%."

"What the hell. This is ridiculous! That's millions in extra costs for us, every year. After such a long relationship with them for years? Should we look for a new money management firm in the States?" Shafi banged his glass on the table.

"Easy, Shafi, easy. I felt angry, too. But that's not the point I'm coming to—him asking for a fee increase and me getting poisoned. These events can't be unrelated. One of our competitors has planned to screw us on various fronts. He wants to hit our finances by influencing Rock & Apostle. At the same time, he wants to behead our organization by offing me. I'm sure he would have a presence and influence in Mumbai, too."

Assisted by Ravi's brain, Tej wove the perfect story, shaping the narrative and leading towards the path where he wanted to direct Ravi's resources.

Shafi was playing with the dial of his wrist-watch. "Hmm. Which is why you directly came here from the airport instead of going to your mansion in the city?"

"Yes."

"Who would want to off you, boss? Tarneja? Wadia? Russell?" Rujeeth was worried, too. They already had a lot of enemies in this trade; they couldn't afford a new one.

"No, Rujeeth. These people, they hate me all right, but they don't have the guts to go this far. We need to find this man. I need the best of our investigators to work with me on this. Can you ask Kevin Sharma and his team to report to me for the next few days? I want them here as soon as possible." Kevin Sharma was the lead detective in Ravi's organization. His team was often used to investigate and locate high profile targets for the gang.

Shafi revolted. "They'll work out of here? Their whole team? But we can't just move them out of their current assignments and reassign them to this witch hunt."

"We can and we will re-assign whomever we need," Tej cut off Shafi. "Don't you think this is the highest priority now? And is it too difficult for you to get another team for our normal business affairs? Kevin is the best, and I need him."

Shafi nodded.

"I have specific tasks for both of you. Rujeeth, I want the mercenaries on our payroll well fed, well paid, and ready with their toys. Assemble a small army if you have to. They should be in a flexible location, ever-ready to move on my command. Shafi, get our aviation folks geared up. Our choppers should be repaired, fueled, and ready to be wheels-up at a short notice. I don't want any repair nonsense."

"You are getting ready to fight a full-fledged war, boss. What's the matter?" Shafi trivialized the discussion. He understood the importance of the situation but felt that Ravi was making it far more serious than it was. It was not the first time a rival gang had made an attempt on Ravi's life.

"You think I am overreacting?"

"No…I didn't mean that," Shafi stammered.

"Someone poisoned me, dammit! Do you have any idea how that felt? To lay there helpless, clutching my chest? Pulled closer to death inch by inch? I would have died for sure. I was lucky to have survived that heart attack. But I don't want to leave matters to luck anymore. I don't want to stay a target for my enemies to hunt. Instead, I want to be a hunter. Whomever this son of a bitch is, I will locate him, confront him, and garrote him with my own bare hands.

"But what he pulled off wasn't easy. He's a powerful player. He won't be taken down without careful planning and effort. We need everything we have to stomp the head of this snake. If any of you don't want to be a part of this, I'll understand. I can manage this on my own. But I want both of you on my side. Are you with me on this?"

"Yes, we are," both of them spoke instinctively and with rigor. Their boss was passionate about this, and there was no other choice than to align with him.

Tej couldn't believe what he had just pulled off, with help from Ravi's brain. He realized his aides had their doubts, but he was able to align them with his plan. The first part of his plan was over. Now, a harder problem stared him in the face—how to find Kumbh.

Rujeeth and Shafi left the bungalow, and Tej retired

to his study. He powered up the laptop. It was time for him to delve into another fascinating marvel built by the modern human, the internet. He knew that Kumbh would have acquired a host with wealth, influence, a societal standing.

He started searching for news websites. He was looking for any celebrity, actor, a politician who had experienced an accident, or a sudden dangerous medical condition in the past three days. Time was running out, and he knew he was looking for a needle in the haystack, but he had no other choice.

For dinner, he took a light rice-based meal. After that, he retired all the servants and kept surfing through the internet for a few hours until he dozed off.

Day 4 of 7

13
THE BURDEN OF A HUNDRED GENERATIONS

ej woke up at 8 AM and felt the need to get ready. At least, that was what his host's brain was telling him to do. He showered, put on a red polo t-shirt and his favorite denim jeans, and came to the dining area. There he received a welcome as if he were a king arriving for a feast.

The dining table was full of American, Indian, and Continental food choices. A whole team of chefs and butlers stood on the sides, waiting for orders. His instinct was to ask for a cheese omelet, sausages, and his favorite rum cappuccino—Ravi's usual favorite breakfast. But Tej stuck to cereals, fruits, and cold milk.

At 08:30 AM, a team of private investigators led by a smart young man named Kevin Sharma arrived at the bungalow. Kevin was a well-groomed man in his late twenties. He had well-combed hair and flaunted expensive eye-glasses. He wore a clean white t-shirt, ironed trousers, and shining shoes. The way he addressed Ravi showed that he both respected and feared the top boss.

Rujeeth had already briefed Kevin's team on Ravi's poisoning incident on the plane. This information helped the team do some prep work before they came to the bungalow. Tej believed this heads-up made their job somewhat easier, or so he thought. He asked them to take one of the big, empty rooms in the bungalow and set up a control station there.

Ravi sat with Kevin. Kevin took out a thin docket of papers from his leather bag, showed it to Ravi, and started to explain.

"Sir, our team started our research yesterday itself. This morning, while we were traveling to this place, I printed out a complete list of people who could have a hand in this attempt on your life. The names on this list are rank-ordered in priority of the most probable culprits. The topmost name is Dhanraj Bargadia, a.k.a. D.B.. He owns multiple factories, warehouses and construction business in Mumbai, Pune, and surrounding areas. We have used some of his facilities previously to ship some of our contraband. The next on the list is…"

"Wait, let me read it myself," Tej cut Kevin off and took the list from him. Kevin handed over the sheet of paper to Tej. The sheet had thirteen names printed on it. He read those names.

Could one of them be Kumbh's new host? No. Tej reasoned with himself. There was no reason that Kumbh would have taken a host in one of Ravi's enemies. While it was a remote possibility, that line of investigation was digressive.

Tej recollected his previous night's internet search— anyone influential who had experienced an accident, medical condition or such incident in the past three days. He was sure that was a much better line of inquiry.

Though he himself couldn't find anything on the internet, smart investigators could dig out better clues if they pursued the right search parameters.

While he was brooding, Kevin's words broke his chain of thought. "What happened, sir? Does this list look like a good starting point to you?"

Tej looked at Kevin, and instantly he knew what the right words were to direct him onto the path to Kumbh. Ravi's brain was at play.

"Kevin, buddy. Whomever this guy is, he was only inches away from taking my life." Kevin was nodding as Ravi spoke. "I am damn serious when I say that I want to teach this bastard a lesson at any cost. I'm sure you share my enthusiasm and will do your best to help me nail this son of a bitch."

"Absolutely, sir."

"The list you gave me, it's awesome. I love the work you guys have done to prepare this. But please keep this list in your back pocket for now. This man we're looking for is very smart. I am afraid your conventional investigative processes won't help us here. We need to think outside the box. Can you do that for me?"

"Yes, sir."

"Good. I will give you certain specific search parameters, and want your team to dig names out using those parameters."

"Sure, sir. We are at your service."

"I want you to start with making a list of all influential people in Mumbai. I want film actors, politicians, and businessmen. Anyone in town with money and muscle, who have experienced a shocking incident in the past five days."

"A shocking incident?"

"Yes—any kind of assassination attempt, any freak accident, any sudden medical condition. Even if they so much as fainted and recovered. Collect this data for the past five days. Can you get it?"

"We can. But that is a rather peculiar ask, sir. Do you know anything which we don't know? Or have you received a tip to make you ask for something this specific? And if so, we would like to know the exact wording, or get a text or audio file of that tip. Sometimes, that helps us unearth clues."

"Call it a divine tip. A gut feeling which I want you to pursue."

"Sir, I would again advise us to start from the list I prepared."

"Kevin?"

"Yes, sir."

"I don't like to repeat myself." Tej looked at him right in the eye. It was Ravi's characteristic grim glance, which was enough to scare those who worked under him to death.

Kevin's face turned pale as he gulped and muttered, "Sure, sir. Your orders are noted. We're on it, right away."

Kevin huddled with his team of analysts and hackers in the room, then dialed in his on-the-street hires over a secure teleconference bridge.

Tej took a deep breath and felt like smoking a cigarette. He actually lit one, owing to Ravi's muscle memory, but decided not to smoke it. Ravi's body was craving a puff but Tej found the whole idea of inhaling poisonous air reprehensible. He was reminded of the Aghoris in his village, who used to smoke some kind of narcotic in a pot, and used to throw out thick smoke-cloud from their nostrils. Because of Aghoris, his chain of thought led to the memory of his visit to the queen of necromancers.

The meeting with Rudrakshini started playing in front of his eyes. A few days ago, he was just a common man. He was a villager who sat in his bamboo-hut, teaching his friend Manu Kumar how to tie a string to a bow. Yet today, he was sitting in the distant future, undertaking a pursuit he couldn't have fathomed even in his distant dreams. He felt too far from what he used to be.

"Sir." Kevin had returned to him.

"Yes, Kevin?" Tej responded with a poker face.

"Sir, I wanted to say that we need time to set up our equipment. We have a lot of folks on the ground as well, with whom we will coordinate from here to get intel. I'll keep updating you with what we find according to your search parameters. Meanwhile, you can take rest. Rujeeth Sir said you were not feeling well yesterday."

"I will only rest when I find our Mr. X," Tej quipped, but he realized his presence in that room was making the whole team nervous. He got up and walked towards the door, but another fact struck him. After taking a new host, Kumbh would have moved to a fortified location and ensconced himself. Kevin's team also needed to consider this. He turned around and addressed the team.

"Folks, add one more constraint to your search. Filter for people who left the city after their revival from the incident they experienced. These people should be high on your priority list. Am I clear?"

"Yes, sir," all of them said in unison as if they were soldiers responding to their general. Tej walked out.

Now that the investigating team had gone to work, Tej knew he had another essential task to finish—a task which was pivotal to his entire plan. He had to get hold of Rudrakshini's sacred green bhasm powder, needed for the demon invocation spell. He had already enquired from his close aide Naahan the location of the ancient temple in Bhramatipura. There, he would find the vaahak clan and the temple where Guru Rigu would have hidden the sacred bhasm with vaahaks.

He had also asked Naahan to have a small team ready to leave at any moment. Naahan had been Ravi's loyal bodyguard for many years. Tej liked him because he followed instructions without asking too many—rather, any—questions.

Within thirty minutes, Tej, Naahan and ten trained commandos in plainclothes left for Bhramatipura. The place was roughly two hundred and fifty kilometers from his bungalow, and the expected journey time was four hours. The thought of sending one of his men to get the bhasm did cross Tej's mind, especially given the actual danger to his vessel's life. Still, he recalled how Guru Rigu himself had gone to fetch the bhasm the last time. It was an activity he felt he should trust no one else to undertake. His whole plan of taking Kumbh back centered on that small object.

It was late afternoon when they reached Bhramatipura. They took one more hour to locate the temple grounds, a small but famous temple of Lord Shiva. Tej asked Naahan and his security detail to wait outside while he removed his shoes and went inside.

He asked for the head priest and met him. The head priest was a man of sixty-five, named Ramanujam. He was frail, with a weak, wrinkled body, and his forehead bore a thin layer of sandalwood paste. Tej enquired with

Ramanujam about an ancient wooden box, which he was there to fetch.

For a couple of seconds, the old man gave Tej a look of disbelief. He then took him to a small room and started fumbling through his old books. After dusting and the reading covers of a few of them, he finally selected an old book. Most pages of this old book were carefully preserved in plastic wraps.

Ramanujam spoke in a shaky voice. "Yes, we are descendants of the ancient vaahak clan. Our ancestors foretold that a traveler from another world will come to ask for this artifact one day, and we have to keep it safe. No one knew about it except the head priest, who was my father, and before him, his father and so on. We believed it was only a story, like many others, but we kept this story close to our hearts, like a family secret.

"This artifact, this wooden box you are asking for, has stayed safe in our temple's inner sanctum for ages, wrapped inside a cloth. No one even dared to look at it, ever. This is one of the ancient notebooks written by our forefathers. It mentions the exact date the traveler would come, which was yesterday. I had been waiting for my whole life for yesterday. I spent the whole day yesterday in anxiety, praying to the lord. I expected that the traveler would come, and no one came. I concluded no one ever would."

"And here I am." Tej smiled. He was a little amused at the perplexed expressions on the old priest's face. But beneath this mirth, he also harbored anxiety about getting hold of that bhasm and heading back to Mumbai.

"And here you are. But this book also talks about something else." The priest tried to hint at what he was looking for without giving it away.

"A verse from Shiv Mahapuraan, right?" Tej quipped, and the priest nodded in affirmation. He assured him that the right person was seeking the artifact and not some imposter. He recited the complete verse taught to him by Guru Rigu with as much articulation as possible.

Ramanujam made him recite the verse at least five times before he could believe it. He then asked him to wait in that room while he went inside the inner sanctum of the temple. He took a good thirty minutes, while Tej eagerly waited outside.

Ramanujam came out with a dusty, medium-sized wooden box. He opened it, and inside was an object wrapped in a rugged red cloth. Removing that cloth revealed another smaller, round, dark brown wooden box. The box had its lid sealed. Tej recognized the box—the same one in which Rigu had placed the powder.

At that moment, Tej felt strong respect for Ramanujam and the vaahak clan of priests. His image of this future was that of a ruthless world, a place full of people ready to deceive, hurt and kill others for money and power; a realm full of beings who knew no principles, followed no ethics or morals. But these priests had dutifully and selflessly preserved a small object for thousands of years—not for any benefit, but out of the respect of their traditions. They did it to venerate the rules established by their elders. While it was easy for him to take Vaahaks for granted, it was an immensely difficult job to keep a small object such as this safe for such a long time. It was a burden which thousands of generations of vaahaks shared.

With trembling hands, the priest handed over the small box to Tej. Tej's throat was too heavy to say any words of thanks, but his face conveyed the gratitude. He knew he had to check the contents before he could leave that place.

He asked the priest for a moment alone, took out a Swiss Army knife from his pocket, and cut through the clay seal. Beneath the seal was the tricky maze of wooden levers and blocks which Rigu had taught Tej how to solve. After sliding a few small wooden bars and sticks on top of the box, the inner lid clicked open. When he opened the box, he smiled. The sparkling green bhasm powder was in there, intact—the same bhasm which Rudrakshini showed him when he met her thousands of years in past, two days ago.

While touching the box, he had noticed the surface of the box was rough on one side. He took a small handkerchief and wiped out dust from that area. Someone had inscribed a Sanskrit writing on the box. With some difficulty, he read it. It said "Samarth Bhasin." *Samarth Bhasin? Why would Guru Rigu write these words on the box?* That read like a name of a person.

He closed the box and covered the maze-lid again with clay. He stepped outside the room, touched the priest's feet, and took his blessings. The priest had tears in his eyes and a smile on his face as if a mountain's worth of weight was lifted off the old man's shoulders. Generations of pledges their family took as vaahaks had been fulfilled today.

Tej asked if the words "Samarth Bhasin" meant anything to him, but the priest was clueless. He assured Tej that no one in their family ever touched the inner box; engraving anything on it was out of the question. Tej said his goodbyes and left the temple. The entourage started for Mumbai.

But this day would not end without a few more

surprises. As they embarked on their return journey, they received intel from Kevin and his sources. The team had intercepted another threat. One of the rival cartels was planning another attempt on Ravi's life, somewhere along the Mumbai Pune Expressway. This was a problem because now they would have to completely avoid the highway, and travel through the maze of half-built village roads. They would have to take a lot of long detours before they reached Mumbai.

This new route plan and proposed delays annoyed Tej, but with the sacred bhasm in hand, he wanted no complications, so he agreed to the longer route. Throughout the return journey, Tej held the wooden box close to him. He concealed it in a small black leather bag which he kept clenched in his hands. The name "Samarth Bhasin" echoed in his mind. Could this person lead him to Kumbh? Or was it the name of Kumbh's new host? Should he call Kevin and ask him right away?

He decided against it. He wanted to wait until he reached the bungalows. In the wee hours of the morning, they finally arrived at his bungalow.

Day 5 of 7

14
TRIANGULATING THE DEVIL

t 06:37 AM, the caravan entered the bungalow's premises. Tej was fatigued and sleepy, but he headed to the control room straightaway. He was eager to meet Kevin and check the team's progress in finding in Kumbh's new host.

When he entered the control room, he realized that Kevin's team had fully set up the room. Various large and small computer monitors, laptops, and other gadgets were placed all around. Several screens were running live camera feeds of various traffic junctions. Kevin's team was also monitoring surveillance footages from safe-houses of Ravi's known enemies. A few analysts sat glued to their laptops, listening to pre-recorded and live calls. A group of investigators leafed through dark-net chatrooms for any heavy arms activity undertaken in the past five days. They were looking at any angle they could, chasing clues in most improbable of the locations.

But this fancy setup somehow did not impress Tej. Running a huge empire of arms smuggling required a leader's brain and aptitude, which Ravi had developed over the years. Ravi's brain was telling Tej that the room, although looked busy and productive, had low energy. Most of these folks had been working for over eighteen hours at stretch. Some had been taking a lot of caffeine and smoking to keep themselves up. Although Tej did not want them to stop, he realized that for them to be functioning at their best, he needed to give them a break.

He asked Kevin to send some early starters out for a rest. Those who joined the investigation later in the day could continue working. He then called everyone's attention and addressed them.

"Time out, guys, time out. I know we're all brilliant chaps here, and are putting in our best efforts. I want those of you who started their day early to take a four-hour break. Try to get some sleep, you all. We have enough rooms in this mansion for you to crash in. Ask the housekeeping staff, and they will guide you. Kevin, walk with me outside, will you?"

Kevin and Tej stepped outside. Tej dug his gaze into Kevin's eyes but kept quiet. Kevin looked at him for a moment, then fumbled. "Sir, today we focused on your search parameters, but …"

"But what?"

"But we were side-tracked a bit because we received a tip on another attempt on your life."

"All right, I'm not leaving this bungalow anymore. I am safe and sound here, so you can ignore any such further tips. Can you please focus on finding who is actually behind this rather than getting side-tracked?"

"Sure, sir."

"During whatever time you could devote today to my search conditions, what did you find?"

"Sir, we have identified a list of seventeen individuals

in Mumbai who fit your criteria. They all are celebrities or well-known powerful figures. Each of them underwent a life-shaking incident in the past five days. All have recovered from that and are now doing better."

"Did any of them move to a secure location after their recovery?"

"That is the part of the information we are still working on. We are going through flight plans for private jets that left Mumbai within the past five days. Registered ones are easy to get, but unregistered ones will take time, as we need to obtain them by other means. We are also looking at traffic cam feeds of major junctions throughout the city. If a big convoy of cars or private trucks left the city in the past five days, we will know."

"All right, take a break. After the team is back, I need a status update report every two hours."

Kevin went into the room, and Tej headed to his private suite.

His whole body ached with pain because of lack of sleep and the tense journey. The last four days had been very eventful for him. He felt as if every last bit of energy in his body had been drained out. He entered his suite and looked at his hand-tufted cashmere-blend mattress. It was one of the most comfortable beds he had ever slept on, but he still missed sleeping on the bed made of bamboo and jute back in his village. That bed used to be his eventual comfort after hectic farm duties or a tiring day of panther hunting. He set an alarm for five hours later on his phone and crashed on his bed.

The alarm broke his sleep exactly five hours later, at noon. He got up, took a shower, changed, and went straight to the control room. He realized that people were already back on their stations. Kevin, too, had returned and was having a discussion with a few members of his team, sipping from a coffee mug. As soon as he saw Tej, he came over and handed him over a sheet of paper, on which three names were typed, along with some details.

"These are the names we have shortlisted, sir. There is a very high chance that our target is one of these."

Tej started to read the detailed descriptions of those names.

First was a famous real-estate builder, Shaukat Ali Tyrewala, forty-three years old. He had been shot in broad daylight four days and thirteen hours ago. He'd suffered multiple gunshot wounds and was rushed to the emergency room. When doctors checked him, his pulse was momentarily gone, but they were able to resuscitate him. He was awake for a few moments but again slipped into a coma. After twelve hours, when he again came to his senses, his team shifted him to an unknown location.

The second was Narendra Moreen, a well-known stock trader, and money launderer. He was working at his morning job when he'd been stabbed seven times in stomach by an assailant. This incident took place around four days and eight hours ago. Narendra was rushed to the hospital where he was saved after thirteen hours of complex surgery. He was currently in the hospital, and was alive but unconscious.

The third was Juniata Gonzalez, fifty-seven years old, a seasoned politician. She was a member of the Goa legislative assembly and was in Mumbai for a party meeting. She suffered a massive cardiac arrest while having breakfast around four days and two hours ago. Her staff had rushed her to a nearby hospital, where doctors stabilized her. Later, her staff took her back to Goa.

Below those three names, there were three more names. These were similar cases, but Kevin believed they did not quite meet the search parameters. A famous model in her early twenties had been acid-attacked by her stalker while she was returning from a photoshoot. A well-known businessman in his late forties had been attacked by a pack of ravenous stray dogs while he was jogging. At last, there was a drug dealer who was badly injured in a hit and run but succumbed to his injuries soon after. Having looked at the complete list, Tej was not satisfied. Something was amiss.

"Kevin, does the name 'Samarth Bhasin' ring a bell?"

"Samarth Bhasin?" Kevin sifted through several sheets of paper for this name. "Yes, sir, Samarth Bhasin was one out of our seventeen names. But we filtered him out because he did not survive his accident."

Wow, that can't be a coincidence. Tej thought.

"You filtered him out because he did not survive? Are you sure he didn't? Tell me more."

Kevin signaled another analyst, who handed him a fresh print out, from which he started to read. "Samarth Bhasin, sixty-two years old, a powerful businessman and mafia boss of a major drug-dealing operation. An uncontrolled car nailed him outside his house four days and ten hours ago. He was rushed to the Intensive Care Unit, where they tried to revive him. But his heartbeat stopped, and the pulse was gone. After a few attempts to revive him, they declared him dead."

Tej had a strong feeling that Samarth Bhasin was

Kumbh. His hypothesis was that after his travel to the future, Rigu's visions would have updated, and he would have somehow found out Kumbh's current host. Rigu knew Tej would come to fetch this box and put this name as a message. This was a strong sign, but Tej had to make sure it was an accurate one.

"Kevin, can you dig deeper on this name, please?"

"Sure, but…"

"But what, Kevin?" Tej thundered. He was not in a mood to entertain frivolous questions or suggestions. "Do you think the man we are looking for is so naive that if he is planning to hide, he will make it any easier for us to track him? Just because the hospital declared Samarth Bhasin dead does not mean that he is dead."

Kevin was silent. But Tej wasn't assuaged by his silence.

"Where is Bhasin's dead body? Which mortuary, which body-sheath number, in which hospital? Which doctor declared and signed off on the time of death? Was the body handed over to the family? What proof do we have that Samarth Bhasin is dead? If you can't find these simple details, buddy, then let me tell you, I'm disappointed in you. In that case, I should have had another team look into this. You better pack up."

Kevin felt offended about being reprimanded in front of his whole team. He and his team were investigators who relied completely on logical fact-finding and deductive reasoning. Contrary to their work protocols, they had been chasing weird ghost-tails on Ravi's strange requests, and now they were being chided for not pursuing one particular name—a name which didn't meet Ravi's own initial search parameters.

Tej sensed the look of indignation on Kevin's face.

He himself was tired and agitated, but this was not a time for him to antagonize the team. The stakes were too high for him to weaken their motivation and jeopardize this search. He took a deep breath. "I'm sorry for the outburst, Kevin. I trust you and the team. I am relying on you to do the right thing. But in return, I want you to trust my instincts, too. I have been in this game for too long. I know a dark shadow when I see it."

Ravi was their top boss, and he'd apologized for his outburst, which was a big deal for him. Kevin had not worked directly with Ravi in the past, but he had known Ravi to be a strict task-master. This apology was something Kevin did not expect. Kevin felt relieved and motivated by these words.

"It's all right, sir. We understand you want this man at any cost, which is why you are being hard on us."

"Good. I want every resource, every asset we have, to focus on Samarth Bhasin. Forget everything else. I want even the minutest details on him. Time is running out for us, so be honest with me, Kevin. Can you do this?"

"Give me two hours, sir. If this Samarth Bhasin is alive, we will lay his entire history and geography out before you."

"All right. You know where to find me." Tej patted Kevin's shoulder and left.

Two hours later, at around two in the afternoon, Kevin sent a message, and Tej returned to the control room. Kevin was ready to give him an update.

"I'm all ears, Kevin."

"You were bang on right, sir. Samarth Bhasin is alive!

After he was hit by the car, his men rushed him to the hospital. He was declared dead on arrival. That was the actual entry recorded in the hospital's register. But two of our field agents rounded up the doctor who wrote that entry. We also got hold of three nurses who were present in that operating theatre. After a few threating words, they narrated the whole story, and the story is very interesting. After two minutes of staying dead, Samarth Bhasin not only recovered but also miraculously came out of the coma. He then forcefully insisted on leaving the hospital. The hospital staff was paid heavily to keep quiet about the fact that he has survived."

"That's good, Kevin, excellent. What happened after that?"

"After that, within the next two hours, he also chartered a convoy of three military-grade helicopters and left Mumbai. His destination was his small privately-owned island in the Indian Ocean, called Macci-Pulau. This is a deserted island declared unsafe for tourist travel."

The pieces of the puzzle were coming together for Tej, but he wanted to be accurate about this. He recalled Rigu's initial words to him. When Rigu told him about Kumbh's escape for the first time, he said, *"Today at 6 PM Eastern time in 2024 AD…"*

That's it. That was the time when Kumbh escaped.

Kevin saw a kind of a flash in Ravi's eyes and realized he was onto something.

"Kevin, what is 6 PM eastern in our time?"

"That would be 03:30 AM India time, sir."

"And when was Samarth Bhasin revived?"

"It was around this time, sir."

"Are you sure, Kevin? I don't want approximations. I

want certainty."

"Absolutely certain, sir. Our agents have also obtained the scanned copy of the hospital logs, and have sent that to us on messenger. The attending nurse herself wrote this note. I can show it to you." Kevin showed him a scanned note on his phone. "Doctor declared time of death at 03:29 AM. The patient recovered at 03:31 AM. This second part around his recovery was later redacted, sir."

Tej smiled. Finally, the pieces of the puzzle had come together, and the picture was perfectly clear. At 03:30 AM India time, the Virtexo developers uploaded the patch, and Kumbh escaped the time-prison. Right after that, he undertook the knock-off blitz and finally took up residence within the body of a man called Samarth Bhasin at 03:31 AM.

Bhasin was an individual with the wealth and political connections to game the system. Hence, Kumbh had used his resources to charter helicopters and escape to a secured private island. There, he could live out his seven days in this time-slice with peace.

Tej felt ecstatic and thanked God. A small detail given by Guru Rigu had finally led him to Kumbh. There was no doubt in his mind that Samarth Bhasin was Kumbh.

"Kevin, this Samarth Bhasin, he's our guy."

"But how, sir? What am I missing here? How is 03:30 AM time relevant?"

"You did an awesome job. Don't worry about anything else. Now you have another important task. I need complete details on the island Samarth Bhasin has traveled to. I also want naval intel and satellite imagery from the adjoining islands. And yes, this information will not leave this room. Understood?"

"Yes, sir."

"Get Shafi and Rujeeth on a telephone line right away."

Within two hours, by around 4 PM, Shafi, Rujeeth, and seven other top members of their gang had reached Ravi's bungalow. They sat in a huge conference room for the next few hours, strategizing their next steps. The target was Samarth Bhasin, and he was to be dealt with on the highest priority. All this while Kevin's team supplied them with incoming intel on regular basis. During this time Rujeeth was also coordinating their weapon and manpower arrangements.

At around 11 PM they finally had complete details about the island. Macci-Pulau was the island near Indonesian waters where Samarth Bhasin had holed himself up. He was reportedly hiding in an old castle named *Taiyō-jō*, Japanese for Sun-Castle.

Rujeeth also provided an update—he had assembled a small army along with several choppers and heavy artillery. In fact, as he spoke, the war machinery and men were being moved to another abandoned island called Mehu-dweep. This island was two hundred and twenty-five kilometers away from Macci-Pulau and would be used as the base of operations to launch an offensive.

Tej had been only listening to these conversations and plans for past few hours, rarely interjecting. As a result, he was bathed in an information overdose.

Everyone in the room had been munching snacks and cold drinks being served by the bungalow's catering staff. But the discussions had been heavy for them. Planning an offensive such as this, in a matter of hours, was no mean task.

As Rujeeth got off his last phone-call for the day, he threw his phone on the table. He poured an expensive eighteen-year old scotch in his glass and raised it to make a toast. "To operation North Eagle! Let's catch this son-of-a-bitch, Samarth Bhasin!"

Tej gave a fake smile and raised a glass of water. "To operation North Eagle!"

"What boss? Only water, no drinks? This is not a time to go sober. We got our guy, and we will nail his ass. This is the time to celebrate." Rujeeth chuckled.

"We haven't got him yet. I will only celebrate when I strangle that bastard with my own hands."

"Okay, boss, suit yourself." Rujeeth took a deep sip.

"Have a drink or two if you want, but no one is getting drunk tonight," Tej declared, addressing them. All the associates in the room, who were getting ready to relax after a few hours of intense meetings, stiffened in their seats. "I want you guys to take a brief rest, after which we should be ready to leave. Any of you has questions?" Tej declared.

"No questions, boss, we are good to go." Shafi who had just poured himself a glass of expensive wine set the glass back on the table.

"Rujeeth, what is the earliest we can leave?"

"The chopper is ready, boss; we can leave as we wish. It will take us to the airport, and from there on we have our private jet ready to take us to our destination." Rujeeth set his half-emptied glass on the side.

"And refresh my memory—where exactly are we going again?"

"Mehu-dweep, an island in the Indian ocean. We have

used it a few times, and believe me, it's a perfect spot. It will be our base of operations."

"All right, friends, we will be wheels-up in two hours. Eat, drink, shave, shower, relax. Do whatever you want in these two hours. I want everyone at the helipad at exactly 01:00 AM."

Day 6 of 7

15
OPERATION NORTH EAGLE, TARGET YELLOW PRINCE

avi, Rujeeth, Shafi and seven of their associates arrived at the Mehu-dweep airbase at around two in the afternoon. Their aim was to conduct a detailed assessment of soldier preparedness, discuss the strategy of the offensive with military experts, and decide upon execution timelines. The target was Samarth Bhasin, now code-named "Yellow Prince."

As they alighted from the choppers, they were received by an officer named Raatu Kaniago. Kaniago was a forty-year-old ex-Indonesian Navy Commodore who would be the senior team leader, the captain, for Operation North Eagle. Kaniago and his men had readied a huge aircraft hangar, where they'd meet the military team leaders and discuss the nuances.

After a brief initial report by Captain Kaniago, Ravi and team started their inspection. Two hundred mercenaries stood at the hangar, waiting for orders. All of them were in their khaki uniforms, ready to wage a mini-war, and equipped with a full military kit. They had state-of-the-art guns, knives, magazines, bar-mines, and ballistic eye protection. Each of them wore an Mk 6 Helmet fitted with mounted night vision systems.

Five Sikorsky UH-60 Black Hawks and ten CH-47D Chinook helicopters were also fueled and ready to take off with trained pilots. While Black Hawks were well-known for their stealth tech, the Chinooks had been brought in for heavy-duty combat. Seven of the Chinooks were fitted with heavy armaments, such as M60D 7.62×51mm machine guns. The other three had XM159C 19-tube 2.75"-rocket launchers mounted on them.

Seeing the military accouterments in front of his own eyes was revolting for Tej. But he now understood the actual reason behind Rigu choosing Ravi as a host for him. His gang was not only involved in selling munitions but for an ancillary payment, they also arranged for small armies on a lease. These armies could quell major uprisings and subdue small governments. At the helm of this gang, weapons, hired-men, military strategists—in fact, everything "war"—was at Tej's finger-tips.

The junior leads under Captain Kaniago started presenting the weapons and their destructive power. During one such presentation, one of the leads showcased a series of deadly bullets they had recently received. These fragmenting 5.56×45mm bullets not only pierced the skin but broke into shreds at impact. If shot in the head, the bullet would perforate the target's brain in multiple places, leaving no chances of medical recovery.

Tej was appalled, witnessing the enablers of death on a naked display. At what point of time in history did humankind start traversing a path of self-annihilation?

Instead of doing good for the world, humans designed weapons which could decimate populations within minutes.

In his efforts to capture Kumbh, Tej was not sure how many lives they would lose, but a gory war was a cost of the bloodless peace that followed. Tej decided that this was not a time for him to get into a cycle of guilt and self-mistrust. He brutally suppressed the moral conflict within him. He was on a path he knew was righteous, and his only way out of it was to move forward.

Their plan was to leave Mehu-dweep at 02:30 AM the next day, in the dead of the night. That way, they would stay under the radar of coast-guard agencies of most neighboring countries. Once they got in the vicinity of the target island, they would send the first wave of attacks around 03:30 AM. They code-named themselves as "The Green Army."

They had received intel that Macci-Pulau had some strong defensive measures in place. Their eventual target, Samarth Bhasin, the "Yellow Prince," was holed up somewhere in the castle, Taiyō-jō. The castle was not only fortified for an effective defense, but there was also a significant military presence detected around it. Satellite imagery showed at least five anti-aircraft guns and several sniper points. The possibility of hidden landmines could also not be ruled out.

From old schematic maps of the area available, the Taiyō-jō was also known to be a WW II military base for the Imperial Japanese Navy in the Indian Ocean. It was possible that inside the castle there existed an inner sanctum. This sanctum would essentially be a military bunk which would be robust enough to withstand heavy artillery fire. The sanctum might remain unaffected, even if the outer walls of the castle were damaged or demolished. The whole place was ready to withstand a major assault. It was clear that Yellow Prince had left no stone unturned to make sure he stayed unequivocally protected.

After listening to the whole plan, Tej got restless. The simple reason was that the military strategists planned the operation at 03:30 AM the next day. They were inching closer to the sun-set of the seventh day. Tej had wanted the Green Army to attack much earlier than that, but the strategists strongly advised against any rash action. Tej finally had to agree to their timelines. The success of the operation was important, and they were the experts at conducting such offensives.

Tej also laid out some ground rules of his own. He told Captain Kaniago and the strategists that he did not want the castle to be destroyed. He wanted to kill Samarth Bhasin with his own hands. They advised against it, but this was the point Tej was not ready to concede.

Since he was the big boss, the strategists had to change their approach. Now the main aim was not to demolish the castle from a distance. Strategists devised a two-pronged plan.

The first part of the plan was to gain control of the area around the castle. After the soldiers secured the area around the castle, the helicopters were to airdrop the Green Army soldiers on the island and leave.

The second part was infiltration into the castle. This plan was also laid out in detail. The first segment of this plan was to have a team of fifty soldiers called "Team Alpha" gain entry into the castle. Captain Kaniago would himself lead this team. Team Bravo and Charlie, with thirty soldiers each, would remain on standby.

The first entry was to be done in a manner which would avoid any structural damage to the castle. Team Alpha was to gain entry, search the castle, and neutralize any threats inside. If they could avoid major losses to themselves, they were to find the innermost bunker. Their orders were to only locate the Yellow Prince and then inform teams Bravo and Charlie. After that, Team Bravo, led by Rujeeth, was to enter the castle, followed by Team Charlie, led by Ravi.

The preponderant rule was that the Yellow Prince would only be killed either by Ravi or in his direct presence. Otherwise, he was not to be touched. Forces could only arrest him.

After they were done with the Yellow Prince, they were to escape out of the castle and travel on foot to a rendezvous point. This point was fixed as a small clearing in a jungle on Macci-Pulau. This jungle was eight kilometers north of the castle and was a perfect hiding spot. There they were to stay hidden in the dense woods till 10 PM when they were to be extracted.

Tej was not worried about the extraction plan. He knew that once he ran the demon invocation spell on Samarth Bhasin, he would be able to pull Kumbh's consciousness out and take it back to 3057 BC.

Weapons were checked, choppers were inspected, and strategies were finalized. At around 08:00 PM, Ravi and his associates came over to their comfortable camping tents. They planned to relax for a few hours. Tej caught a much needed few hours' sleep, as he wanted his body ready and focused for the planned offensive.

Tej's wrist-watch alarm broke his sleep at 02:00 AM, and he started to get ready for the battle. He wore a bulletproof vest and packed a Glock-19 9mm Semi-Automatic. He also kept one Beretta 92FS, along with several magazines.

Ravi hadn't been a part of the Armed Forces, but he had undergone extensive weapons training, several times, throughout his life. He had also been a part of a few combat missions early in his career. Tej knew this training and experience of his vessel would come handy in this operation.

For Rudrakshini's blood ritual he needed only two things, a knife, and the sacred green bhasm. The knife would also be helpful in one-on-one combat. So he packed Fairbairne-Sykes in a secure sheath in his harness. In his right front pocket, he kept the green bhasm. He had transferred it out of the wooden box to a small easy-to-carry plastic pouch. After careful checks, he took a deep breath and started quietly praying. His lips showed little movement as he chanted the *Maha-mrityunjaya* mantra.

At around 02:15 AM IST Rujeeth came to his tent and said. "Boss, we're ready to roll."

Tej came to the old aircraft hangar where two hundred soldiers had assembled and were ready for orders. They'd donned their full military attire. Ravi, Rujeeth, Shafi, Captain Kaniago and several others took the stage. Tej knew he was expected to make a speech, so he took the microphone in his hands. He himself had rarely given any speeches, but he felt no stage-fright. He had Ravi's brain at his aid. Ravi had been giving motivational, light, and harsh speeches to his staff and his men throughout his life.

Tej eyed the horde of soldiers in front of him, gave a graceful smile, and addressed them. "If some of you are expecting a speech like the one in that movie 'Independence Day', no, I will not do that. We are not going to fight aliens here." The whole crowd laughed. Some of them even whistled and clapped.

"Neither am I going to say any motivational words here. You all are being paid in Krugerrands, so I know your motivations are aligned." The crowd applauded again.

"Nor am I going to bore you with technical terms such as 'we will go in hot', 'high altitude, low open' etcetera. I am sure Captain Kaniago would have briefed you with those terms." The crowd again jeered. Kaniago gave a strange wide-toothed smile.

Tej continued. "But since I am the one paying you sharp mercenaries for this mission, there is one thing I want to make crystal clear. You fight, you shoot, you decimate the targets. But this guy, Samarth Bhasin, he is off limits for you. Each of you has his picture. You know how he looks. Get that picture in your head. You see him running, hiding, doing anything. You will not shoot at him or hurt him. You will do nothing other than arresting him. He is mine. I want him alive! At any cost. Is that clear?" Many in the crowd nodded their heads. They were listening intently.

"Is that clear?" Tej shouted.

"Yes, sir!" A coordinated sound resonated throughout the crowd. They were men of the military, after all; following orders ran deep in their blood. Tej looked at Captain Kaniago and nodded. Kaniago started assigning men to their choppers. The crowd dispersed.

Day 7 of 7

16

ENTERING THE JAWS OF THE DEMON

astle Taiyō-jō itself was an antediluvian structure, but some parts of it had been fortified using huge iron rods and mortar plastering. Four anti-aircraft guns stood on the four corners of the castle. Thirty armed men guarded each of the guns.

A tight watch-guard parameter with a five-hundred-meter radius had been established around the castle. Seventeen watch-towers along the periphery of this zone monitored possible hostile activity. Each watchtower had two soldiers on the top with short-range monitoring telescopes and two trained snipers in an alert stance. Each watchtower was guarded by small teams of five soldiers at its base. One radar station was also established within the parameter to intercept early signals of any air attack.

At exactly 03:34 AM IST the combat began. Two Black Hawks from the Green Army came in undetected, and with an element of surprise, took out two of the four anti-aircraft guns. They also destroyed five of the watchtowers and went away, flying outside the range of rest of the two guns. The on-ground forces reeled from this sudden assault and destruction.

Within a minute, the second major wave hit the castle. Five of the Chinook helicopters came in with heavy artillery fire, annihilating several targets on the ground. They also destroyed eleven more watchtowers and took down one more anti-aircraft gun. But the retaliatory attack this time cost the attacking forces, too. One of the Chinooks was destroyed mid-air, and another took a shot to its rotor, because of which it crashed a few kilometers away.

After several such waves of attacks, the on-ground enemy-targets suffered major casualties. The survivors had no choice but to raise the white flag and surrender. Around one hundred and fifty Green Army soldiers along with Tej and his associates were dropped around the castle. Within one hour, they established their own defense parameter around it.

Forty-seven enemy soldiers, who had survived, were arrested and kept under tight watch. As expected they were all hired guns with no clear idea on whom they were defending. The first part of the plan was complete, although the number of casualties for the Green Army was more than they expected.

Now the second part of the plan, the infiltration, was to be executed. Cutting through the heavy stone brick walls of the castle was a wasteful exercise. The giant metal door, although heavy, was the most vulnerable point of the castle.

The team started to set-up a series of C4 explosives around the main castle door, but they took extreme precautions. Even one misdirected explosion could have brought down the whole castle structure. That went against Ravi's explicit orders.

At around 07:30 AM, the ballistic experts finally okayed the set-up. There was no further activity from inside the castle till that time. Ravi was called to press the "red button," a switch which started the chain of controlled demolitions around the door. The detonation was successful. The entry to the castle was wide open. Tej's hopes were going up. They were ahead of time. But in a battle, when has anything ever gone according to plans?

At 07:50 AM, Captain Kaniago and his Team Alpha of fifty soldiers entered the castle and progressed into the inner gallery ways. They went radio silent, as they had no idea what awaited them inside, and had to tread with care.

Two crucial hours passed by. The clock read 9:50 AM IST. There was no news from Team Alpha. Tej was very agitated. Sunset was predicted at exactly 06:07 PM Indian Standard Time that day. He was about to ask Rujeeth to take Team Bravo inside when they heard a muffled explosion from inside the castle after which they heard sounds of heavy artillery fire. Armed combat had erupted somewhere within the castle. The radio silence was finally broken. Kaniago's crackled voice was heard on the radio.

"We faced a landmine explosion, after which a few enemy soldiers fired at us….We lost many of our men but could neutralize… neutralize the combatants."

"Captain Kaniago, Team Bravo is coming in as a backup," Rujeeth yelled on the radio.

*"Negative, negative. Something strange is attacking us now…
we don't know what…with sharp teeth, it's ripping our soldiers
apart …"*

"What is it, Captain? Describe it for us."

*" …five of us are hidden inside a nook…sniffing us…is
coming for us…bullets not working…"*

There was a strange loud noise, and the radio went
silent. Captain Kaniago had most likely been killed in
action. Rujeeth and Shafi both had petrified looks on
their faces and fear in their eyes. Tej looked at a group
of seven soldiers who were present there. They were the
team leads. Their confidence was shaken too. Facing guns
and soldiers inside was expected, but a strange creature
on whom bullets were not working? None of them had
encountered anything like that.

"Whatever it is, we have to face it. Team Bravo and
Charlie need to go in," Tej declared.

"What are you saying, boss? We don't even know
what we're getting into. We should wait and get more
reinforcements before we go in."

"Reinforcements? We don't have time Rujeeth."

"What's the hurry?" Shafi interjected. "We have
surrounded the castle, and around a hundred men are
guarding the parameter. No one can go out. Let's get
more weapons, more soldiers and then go in all guns
blazing. We don't know what's inside."

"What a brilliant plan, Shafi," Tej mocked. "While we
sit here waiting, how do you not know that another army
commissioned by Samarth Bhasin is not en route to this
place? We have to get inside and finish him right away."

"Why don't we rip apart the whole place? We know
Samarth Bhasin is inside. Let's get the son of the bitch.
I can arrange for a hellfire missile to be fired on the

castle within the next two hours. This whole place would be stones and rubble after that." Rujeeth was getting frustrated with Ravi's strange doggedness over killing Samarth Bhasin in person.

"No. We don't know for sure that Samarth Bhasin is inside. What if he has already escaped? I don't want to leave here with a dilemma over whether my arch-enemy is dead or alive. I don't want to live the rest of my life with a deadly shadow looming over my shoulder. I want proof of death in front of my eyes."

Rujeeth and Shafi both looked at each other.

"I won't go," Rujeeth said with determination.

"Sorry, boss." Shafi nodded his head in negation.

Tej realized everything was falling apart. Each minute the clock was ticking, Kumbh was inching towards a silent victory.

"All right, I will go in myself. I will take a team of thirty men with me."

Tej looked at the seven team-leads and asked them to assemble their best thirty men.

A half hour later, at 10:30 AM, twenty-two soldiers assembled near the radio station, along with three team leads. Rujeeth and Shafi were sitting on small chairs. They had already given up. Tej stood uptight waiting for soldiers to settle.

"If I am not wrong, I asked for thirty. We only have twenty-two here. And where are the other four team leads?" Tej demanded.

One of the team leads stepped forward. "The news has spread, sir, that there is a strange creature inside, on which even bullets are useless. Who would want to go in? Even these twenty-two soldiers gathered here, they are not sure, sir."

"Hmm. So you're afraid?"

"We are not afraid, sir, but we are not foolish either. In a battle, we know who our combatant is. It's another soldier or a machine or another gun waiting for us on the other side. We are trained to fight those dangers. But taking on an enemy without having any understanding of its strengths and weaknesses is foolhardiness. It's the same as walking into the jaws of certain death. Captain Kaniago was the best of us. He went in with fifty men and still was killed in action. What chance does anyone of us have?"

"One million dollars!" Tej screamed. He was thinking on his feet again. He needed this army at any cost.

"What?" Rujeeth questioned.

"Shhh! Be quiet, Rujeeth." Tej angrily signaled Rujeeth to keep his mouth shut. He turned again to the soldiers.

"I offer one million dollars to every soldier ready to go inside with me. This amount will be transferred to any account of your choice, in any bank, in any city across the world. For every person who signs up to go inside with me, I will initiate the transfer for them right here, right now. The money will be credited to that person's account within the next two hours. So, even if I die during the next two hours, that transfer will still go through. But during these two hours, if anyone tries to flee the castle, or abandon the mission, the transfer will be canceled. Shafi will make sure of that."

"What, boss?" Shafi balked. Ravi was shooting mad instructions in thin air and was expecting them to be executed.

"Can you arrange it, Shafi? To have one million dollars transferred to every gentleman who agrees to go inside the castle with me? Can you do at least this for me? And yes, you will get 2% for each successful transfer." Tej wanted to make sure Shafi had skin in the game.

"Whatever you want, boss. I will get on it." Shafi was relieved. Arranging this much money within this timeframe was difficult, but it was a better choice than following Ravi into the pit of death. Plus, he was getting a two percent cut.

Tej faced the soldiers. "Go spread the news of this offer. The clocks read 10:35 AM IST. I will enter the castle at 11:30. If no one else is ready, I will go in alone. The choice is yours."

At 11:30 AM, around forty-three soldiers were ready to enter the castle with Tej. Each of them had shared their bank details with Shafi, who was initiating transfers for them one by one.

A group of fifteen soldiers entered the castle in a vanguard formation, followed by Tej and the remaining twenty-eight men.

They passed through the main gallery-way into the inner chamber of the castle and entered a huge illuminated hallway. A pile of chewed flesh, dismembered organs, and blood-stained ammunition welcomed them. The end of the hallway was dark, the ceiling lights there were destroyed during the gunfire.

There was a sudden growl at the end of the hallway. The soldiers immediately pointed their guns towards the sound. The pungent stink of human fear and sweat filled the hall. Then they saw the shadow of a huge animal walking towards them.

"No one fires," Tej spoke in a hushed tone. "Let us first understand what this thing is," His hunter instincts were driving him.

The beast slowly walked out from darkness into the light and showed itself. It was a twelve-foot-long and seven-foot-high Liother, a hybrid between a lion and a panther. The monster had bloodshot eyes and a wide jaw with knife-sharp teeth. It had dense lion-like gray hair around its face and neck. Its colossal, muscular body was light black in color and had thin gray hair at some places. Its heavy paws had long sharp claws, which could tear through human flesh, bones, and internal organs with ease. Dark stain-lines made of dried human blood were visible on its face. A severed human-arm clasped between its teeth warned them of its ferocity. It was as if the God of Death himself was staring at them.

Each soldier in that hallway was now regretting his decision to sell his life for a million dollars. It was not only death they feared but the ruthless, inhumane way in which it was going to come to them.

Tej noticed that most of the body of the beast was covered with some kind of light, translucent armor. It was evident that bullet-fire would be futile on most of its body surface. Its forehead, face, and some folds where armor plates joined were the only vulnerable points.

At that moment, Tej pictured what was about to go down in that hallway. The beast would attack them. They would fire on it, but its armor would protect it. Within a matter of seconds, the Liother would disembowel at least ten to fifteen of these men. The animal would ravage their fragile bodies with immense speed and veracious blitz. The rest, witnessing this lethal carnage, would flee the scene. Tej's cause would be lost, and Kumbh would win.

But the word "Blitz" suddenly struck him. He recalled Rigu's words. "Kumbh usually goes on a knock-off blitz, where he knocks off the consciousness of several individuals rapidly before he takes a host."

What if he could use the same technique and knock-off this Liother's consciousness for a few moments? If that happened that will help them gain an advantage on the beast. But could he do such a quick jump? Could he even jump in the same time-slice? Why not? As Guru Rigu said, he only had to focus on his destination.

His destination host was not a human this time, it was this Liother, and his destination time was a few milliseconds in past.

The Liother dropped the severed arm down and eyed the soldiers in front of him. The men tightened their holds on their guns, ready to fire, but no one moved even one inch. Liother bent backward a little, about to jump onto them.

Tej decided it was now or never. He chanted his mantra and re-iterated the destination in his mind. He saw himself traveling towards the beast's brain. It worked!

Tej was inside the animal's brain. Although he did not try to read it, all he saw was blood, bones, flesh, and brutality. Liother's old preys, hunting chases in the forest, and the torture it endured at hands of its captors all were coming to Tej. He was being sucked into the enormous web of bestial images inside Liother's brain. He knew he had to get out. He focused on Ravi's brain and traveled back to his body.

He woke up in Ravi's body and realized that Ravi

had collapsed on the floor, but he swiftly aligned his senses and got up. Liother had collapsed, too, and was vigorously shaking its head. The beast's consciousness was indeed knocked-off, but it was returning to its senses. Some soldiers had dared to go near the creature, aiming their guns at it.

"Shoot it in the head, right now!" Tej screamed at the top of his voice.

The soldiers surrounded the beast and unloaded their bullets into its body—forehead, limbs, wherever they could find a chink in the armor.

They waited a few seconds for Liother to show movement. But the creature was motionless. It had succumbed to its injuries.

Tej sat on his knees, panting. This threat was neutralized. But this battle was far from over.

17

THE DOPPELGANGER

he clock read 11:42 AM. Wasting no more time, Tej got his hands on the schematics of the castle and laid them out on the ground.

The inner sanctum was right behind this hallway in which they were standing. He lit up a bright torch and ambled towards the end. He asked the soldiers to stay put. At end of the hallway was a huge steel door embedded between the dense stone wall: the last line of defense between him and Kumbh.

Again it was futile to cut through the stone walls, as they were thick and dense, but it was plausible to cut through the steel door. The team ruled out the usage of explosives because they were now inside the castle. Any detonation near the walls could have caused irreversible structural damage. The only way was to cut through the steel door using a high-power oxy-acetylene torch.

Tej radioed Rujeeth that the situation was under control. He asked him to send a few men inside, along with the necessary equipment. Within a few minutes, two of the men started cutting a man-sized hole into the door. Tej explored alternate routes to the inner sanctum, but there were none. Every other hallway was completely jammed with huge quantities of concrete. Kumbh had adopted a classic defense technique of bolting all inlets but one sealed shut. The one entrance was guarded with every possible resource.

They took over four hours to cut through the thick steel door. It was around 04:03 PM IST when they finally cut out a hole, through which one man could slip in at a time. Tej peeped through that hole and saw a small passage which turned to the right. As per the schematics, the inner sanctum was right after this passage. He breathed a sigh of relief. He had two good hours before sunset in India.

While he was looking at his watch, a damning realization resounded in his head. He recollected Rigu's exact words. *"As soon as the sun sets on his geo-locale on the seventh day, Kumbh will bolt out of 2024."*

Tej hadn't understood the meaning of geo-locales at that time, but equipped with the knowledge of Ravi's brain, he now knew what they exactly were. This island, Macci-Pulau, was not in the same geo-locale as India. The timezone on this island ran one and a half hours before India's time zone. Which meant if the Sun would set in India at 06:07 PM IST, it would set at Macci-Pulau at 04:37 PM IST. Which meant that he had only thirty-four minutes. This miscalculation could have cost him the whole mission. His goal was within reach, yet so far.

He sent five men through the hole in the door to do a quick recon and report back. He checked his front pocket to confirm that he still had the green bhasm secured in the plastic packet. He also re-checked the sharp knife left in a secure sleeve in his left back pocket.

The men returned and signaled that way forward was clear. Tej entered through the hole in the door. He moved towards the innermost reinforced room of the castle where the periphery of the inner sanctum began.

As soon as he entered the last gallery-way, as per his map schematics, he saw another small door at the end of it.

This was it. The innermost chamber. He saw that three security-guards lying on the ground, lifeless. They were most likely Bhasin's men, shot dead by someone. Moreover, the door they were guarding was not bolted, as he expected. It was slightly open, and its outer bolts were scorched. It was clear that someone blasted through the door using a light-explosive charge.

Tej approached the ajar door with caution. He decided he had to enter the inner sanctum on his own. He could not risk taking other men inside. He knew he won't be able to perform Rudrakshini's ritual in front of them. Or worse, they might shoot Samarth Bhasin in the heat of the moment, and inadvertently sabotage his whole plan.

He asked the men to stay at their positions and gave strict orders that no one should come inside without direct, explicit orders. He was about to step inside when he heard a noise from within the room and stalled himself. Someone inside was speaking in an agitated tone.

He peeked inside the door from outside and saw a boy in his late teens standing in an attack stance. The boy was holding some kind of strange-looking, futuristic gun in his hand. This gun was a long, metallic tube with several levers and patches. It had a small loose pouch near the trigger, and a flask containing an orange boiling liquid was attached below the nozzle. The boy was aiming the gun at a person, whom Tej could not see.

Tej paid attention to what that boy was saying. He was fuming in anger and addressing the other person. "Kumbh, you time-demon, do you even remember me? I am Tej. And do you remember the atrocities you heaped upon me and my mother for so many years? I will avenge those today. Be ready to die for those sins."

Tej was taken aback. Why was this kid referring to himself as Tej? Upon that he was also mentioning the atrocities done to his own mother. Who was he?

"This gun from the future is built specifically for demons of time such as yourself. This will extract all the atoms of your consciousness and will imprison them inside this small membrane," the boy warned as he tightened his grip on the gun, ready to fire.

A burst of uproarious laughter emanated from the other side. Whomever this boy was aiming his weapon at was laughing loudly.

"Why are you laughing, you demon?" The boy shouted.

The man repressed his laughter and responded. His voice was heavy. "Kid, this toy you are holding is complete junk. I have seen several of these in the future. It's a satellite-based weapon, which is configured to a particular geostationary satellite from the future. I am not sure how you even brought it to this time-slice. That's commendable. But beyond that, it will not work here. Yet let me show you what will work here—the.22 caliber which I am holding in my hand. It's metal and ballistics and has been working well since the Chinese invented gun-powder. The best part is, this works everywhere, and especially well on human bodies."

At that exact instant, the boy pressed the trigger on his hi-tech gun. The gun whirred, making a loud, shrilling sound and came to a standstill. Nothing happened. The boy frantically pressed the trigger multiple times, but still no result. Suddenly, there were several loud gunshot noises, and the boy's lifeless body fell to the ground. Kumbh had shot him dead.

Tej's heart was beating even faster. He had witnessed Kumbh taking another life. Five soldiers whom he'd asked to stay back came running. They heard the bullet fire, too, but Tej gestured for them to go back. He waited for a few moments and then entered the room slowly, with a tight grip on his shotgun. He was aiming it at the direction of the voice. For a second, he looked at the body of the boy and felt sad for him. He mapped his steps, kept low, and looked for any object to hide behind, in case Kumbh fired on him too.

The room was huge and well-lit. Tej was not expecting this. The walls were painted silver-grey. Several bright white lights on the roof illuminated the whole space. A lot of boxes of food and medical supplies were placed throughout the room as if it was a bunker built to sustain a natural apocalypse. Tej could not see the whole extent of the room because of these wooden boxes, but he knew Kumbh would be somewhere in there.

He heard that heavy voice again. "I sense another presence here. Who are you? Show yourself."

Tej knew that voice came from behind a huge stack of boxes in front of him. He got up with caution and slunk towards the side of the stack. He clasped onto his shotgun, ready to shoot as soon as he stepped out from behind the stack into the open.

"I used all my bullets on that kid. So don't worry. You

can come in peace," The voice said.

"Don't move!" Tej shouted as he jumped out from behind the boxes and aimed his gun. The man in front of him was sitting in a wheelchair. He was Samarth Bhasin.

18
THE LAST LAUGH

ej observed him for a moment. Bhasin was a short man with a fat belly and a rugged face. He wore a white polo t-shirt, blue trousers, a lavish chocolate-brown coat, and thick sunglasses. He was smoking a Cuban cigar with aplomb. An emptied.22 caliber sat on the ground at his side.

"Now, who are you?" Bhasin asked as he puffed out a thick ring of smoke out of his blackened lips.

"I'm Tej, and I am here to take you with me."

Bhasin cackled again and coughed as he laughed. Tej felt bizarre. If Kumbh was in there, he showed no sign of fear.

"Don't conceal yourself, Kumbh, I know you're in there. Hiding, and afraid." Tej maintained a confident demeanor, but his hands were shaking.

Bhasin's coughing subsided. He looked at Tej, chewing his lower lips as if carefully weaving his next words.

"I am not hiding, buddy. I openly declare I am Kumbh, the greatest time-demon ever. Among the people present in this room, I am not the one who is afraid."

"Greatest time-demon?" Tej mocked. "You are sitting

in the vessel of an old man. Did you take this vessel up to garner sympathy? Believe me, I will show you none."

"You are a fool, Tej. This is not three thousand BC. These are modern times. Physical strength doesn't matter as much. What matters is how many resources and machines one has at his disposal. This fortified castle and the army which welcomed you outside, they all were possible because of this vessel, you moron. I did not possess this body to engage in physical combat with my enemies."

"Yet all these resources which this body provided could not protect you, Kumbh. I penetrated all your so-called defenses."

"Commendable job! Do you want daddy to pat your back, son?"

"Don't call me that, I am not your son. I am Tej, son of Dhara."

"Oh yeah, Dhara. She was a lovely broad when she was young. Has she died in the time you are coming from? Anyhow, I don't care. Though the question is, if you are also claiming to be Tej, then who was that kid I shot a few minutes ago? He was also calling himself Tej. Has Rigasur gone so desperate that within one time-slice, he sent two different versions of the same person to capture me? Well, he forgot that I have seen more futures than any of you kids he has or ever will dispatch to fight me."

"I don't know about that. Renowned sage Shri Rigu sent me to capture you."

"Shri Rigu? Renowned sage?" Bhasin again burst into loud laughter and even clapped.

Tej carefully measured his next words. They were both alone in the room, Bhasin was in the wheelchair, and Tej had the gun. He could easily overpower him and cast Rudrakshini's spell. But he had to make sure this was not another of Kumbh's moves. He did not want to waste the spell and the sacred powder on an imposter pretending to be Kumbh. The sweet taste of revenge was so near, yet he needed to take each step with caution. He required more information and he wanted it fast. For that, he needed to continue the conversation. But Bhasin's laughter was bothering him.

"Why are you laughing, Kumbh? Have you lost your senses?"

"Not me. You have lost your senses." Bhasin pointed his finger at Tej. "That scoundrel Rigasur is making a fool out of you innocent time-demons. He is not Rigu, he is Rigasur. Rig-asur—an *asur*, a rakshasa, a demon. He is himself a time-demon. In fact, he is one of the first time-demons, hence the oldest. The first ones to have received the gift of God, or nature, or evolution. Whatever you call it."

"Stop lying through your teeth."

"Oh, am I the liar? Have you not read the texts on ancient time travelers? The lore says almighty Trikaaldevi, the goddess of time, rarely sleeps. She is omnipresent, omniscient, omnipotent and watches over the universe through the minutest of the time-slices. But on rare occasions, when she sleeps, a time-demon is born. Ancient texts say Rigasur was born the first time Trikaaldevi ever slept."

"Whatever!"

"Yeah, whatever. This is just a story. Fiction concocted by primeval men. Same as the fiction fed to you by Rigasur. In his fable, you are the hero, I am the nemesis and he is the hero's munificent, righteous mentor. While you are considering me a villain, the true villain of your story was always standing behind you. We are not different, Rigasur and I. We are both monsters. But I'm more open about who I am, whereas he prefers to stay in disguise."

"You're a lying bastard. Guru Rigu is not a time-demon. He can't be." Tej knew Kumbh would fabricate any story to dissuade him from his cause. Rigu had warned him that this would happen.

"I know I'm wasting my time trying to enlighten you, kid. You won't believe me. Rigasur is a master deceiver and an expert manipulator. Even I and Vetri couldn't recognize him that night when he captured us by deceit. I can't blame you. You are a tiny tot, a quaint, freshly minted time-demon. You are no match for the fallacious world he has constructed around you."

"No, I don't believe you. Now that you know your capture is imminent, you'll say any crap to prevent your exorcism," Tej taunted.

"Exorcism? I like the specific choice of the word. Don't you tell me that Rigasur is planning a necromancy angle on me, using you? The kid I shot, came with a futuristic technology but failed miserably. I am curious to know what has Rigasur planned with you."

"Stop calling him Rigasur. He is no asur, no demon. Guru Rigu is a time-reader."

"Kid, this isn't funny anymore. Wake up. He is not a time-reader, although he may have a few time-readers as his slaves, or disciples, as he likes to call them. By making them read time visions, he tracks the movements of other time-demons, like myself. He has also enlisted loyal, gullible time-demons such as you in his ashram, to aid him in capturing and taking down other powerful time-demons. Who else can know that better than me? I was one of his first disciples. I did similar odd jobs for him. When I refused to be his puppet, I became his foe. He is a team player though. I'll give him that. I, on the other hand, am more of a lone wolf. I play alone, I hunt alone."

Kumbh paused for a moment, reminiscing over a sad memory. "Though I was not always alone. I used to have a partner, my beloved brother Vetri, whom Rigasur captured. With a little help from an eight-year-old you, if I correctly remember."

"And here I am again. This time, to capture you. Guru Rigu may have enabled me to come here, but I am not here on his orders. I am here to avenge my mother."

"Oh, that's the story Rigasur has pumped you with? Filled you with the hatred of revenge? Yes, we enslaved your mother. But did he not tell you that he indirectly sent your mother to spy on me and Vetri, before our men captured her? And what other fibs did he stuff inside your brain? That I will kill a lot of people in the future? Did he tell you what 'he' will do in the future?"

Tej felt the seeds of doubts being sowed inside of him. He did not feel Kumbh was lying. But again, Kumbh was the one who'd tormented him and his mother, made his childhood hell and would have killed him that night. He needed to satiate his perennial thirst for revenge against Kumbh.

"All right, kid. Go ahead. You seem to have a nasty gun in your hands. Pump these bullets in my body. Kill me." Kumbh goaded him.

"Ah, I wish it was as easy. If I fire these on you, it will be a mere delay for you. You will move your consciousness to another body, and I will have a hard time finding you again. Unfortunately, I'm on a clock."

"Keep dreaming, because I am on a clock too. A few more minutes and my time in this realm will be over." Bhasin smiled and took out another cigar from his coat pocket.

Tej knew time was running out, and he was fairly certain that the man in front of him was Kumbh. Even if he wasn't, Tej would have to take a leap of faith here. He would have to administer Rudrakshini's spell.

Tej moved forward and took off Bhasin's sunglasses, but was appalled to see that Bhasin's eyes were severely burnt. In fact, there were no eyes in those sockets, only dead skin.

"What have you done with your eyes?"

A victorious grin swam across Bhasin's face. "What happened? Shocked? Let me explain. When I escaped Virtexo a week ago and entered Samarth Bhasin's body, I knew someone was coming for me. With only seven days left in my future journey, Rigasur would definitely create roadblocks in my voyage to the future. So I used my newfound influence—that is, Samarth Bhasin's influence—and made this fortified castle my home. I was confident that these private armies, huge castle walls, well-laid traps, they would keep me safe. But experience has taught me that even the strongest armor can be pierced through with the sharpest blade. So I took some extra precautions.

"I suspected Rigasur would try necromancy on me, but most necromancy spells built to capture consciousness require eye-contact. So, I played safe. Five days ago, I got my eyes surgically removed. The doctors here are fabulous. Sorry to disappoint you. You were not going to perform any spells here, were you?" Kumbh had a smirk on his face.

Tej was devastated. With Kumbh's eyes gone, he wouldn't be able to look into them, and the spell wouldn't work. His mission had ended in failure just before the culmination. He looked at his watch—it showed only eleven minutes to sunset.

Should I go ahead use the spell? No, I can't. He was reminded of what Rudrakshini had said. *If you fail this aim, then the spell would suck your consciousness from your body and throw it into an abyss. You will never be able to return from that dark pit.*

"Why are you so quiet, son? Within a few minutes, your father will leave you, again, for a distant journey to the future. Say your goodbyes to Daddy."

"You are not my father. You are a vile apparition from my past."

"Stop being a puppet of Rigasur. You are a time-demon! Past, present, and future don't apply to us time-demons. Look at the immense power we have, Tej. Look at me. I have been reading brains and living alternate lives for millennia. My consciousness carries all that information. Omniscience, you see, is not a consequence of immortality, but a mere side-effect of being a time-demon, a time-god."

"I am neither a demon nor a God."

"Are you not? Have you not experienced travel through the black holes? Only a God can enter a black hole and come back. Looks like you have a lot to learn about yourself, about our species. Let me educate you, kid. We time-demons have been using these black holes to travel through space and time, ever since we knew they existed. My first time-jump happened thousands of years ago. But I can never forget that first lunge towards that supermassive black hole."

Kumbh blabbered incessantly while Tej was counting every passing second. He knew Kumbh was only wasting his precious time. His enemy, the devil of his life, was right in front of him. Yet he stood there, powerless. He had run into a barrier he never anticipated. His mind was blank now.

"Oh, Tej, I cannot describe that feeling in words. As I was being sucked into that giant vortex at such a staggering velocity, it petrified me to the core. But boy oh boy, when you cross the event horizon, your view of the universe transmutes. From the inside, the black hole is actually a giant three-sixty degree spherical lens. It offers infinite doors to countless realms. It has absorbed so much light that it contains a tremendous amount of information about the universe. Past, present, and future, all three of them co-exist in this surreal space, together. You must ..."

"Keep quiet, will you?" Tej shouted. He could not think of anything with this constant drivel pounding his ears.

"You didn't like me educating you? I can understand. Kids usually find their parent's valuable teachings useless." Kumbh was offended. "Let me tell you another story which will interest you. Some details about your mother, which you won't know. She was terrific in bed. Me and Vetri, we took turns on her."

"Shut up, you bastard!" Tej screamed.

"No, no, you need to hear the details of our first night with her. When we removed her clothes the first time..."

"You son of a bitch!" Tej struck Bhasin's face with the butt of his shotgun and knocked him unconscious. "Thank God, you won't utter another evil word," Tej murmured to himself.

He sat near Bhasin's body and started thinking. Kumbh was definitely trying to buy time. But why? Why distract him at this moment when he knew he had won? Why this diversion? Was there another way for Tej to cast the necromancy spell? Maybe getting his own eyes removed was just a false distraction created by Kumbh to dissuade Tej from using the spell.

All these were only speculations. Time was running out. His watch showed four minutes to sunset. With no other alternatives left, Tej decided to go ahead with the spell. He took out the sacred green powder and smeared his right palm with it. Then he started chanting the demon invocation mantra given to him by Rudrakshini. Simultaneously, he took the knife and sliced his powder-smeared palm. His palm bled. He did the same thing with Bhasin's right palm and clasped both of them. Blood connect was established. Kumbh's consciousness was in Tej's control now.

But eye-connect was part of the ritual too. It was essential for their senses to align so that both of them can travel to the past together. Without that the spell was incomplete.

While Tej was trying to rack his brain for ideas, he recalled the Aghori from his childhood, who performed an exorcism. He remembered that the Aghori touched his forehead to the subject's forehead. He also remembered the moment right before the commencement of his time travel to 2024 AD—Rigu had applied sandalwood paste onto his forehead.

Maybe these activities were not mere rituals but had an actual scientific meaning? What if a forehead was in a way a door for consciousness to travel out of the brain into the time-realm? If the sight is a sense, then the touch is a sense, too.

He knew what he had to do. He took some leftover powder and smeared it on his forehead, then smeared some of it on Bhasin's forehead. He touched his forehead to Bhasin's and kept reciting the mantra. He couldn't know for sure if the spell had worked or not.

After a few recitations, Tej decided he had to begin his journey to the past. He focused on the picture of Rigu's chamber, his original anchor. Ravi Kumar Cheri's body fell to the ground like a dead tree. Tej was traveling back to the year 3057 BC.

19
A DARK DECEPTION

Tej woke up in his own body in the Chamber of Time-Travel. He gathered his senses and looked around in haste. Rigu, who was meditating on a seat nearby, opened his eyes and came running to him. Tej looked at the body of Kumbh, which showed no movement.

"I could not capture Kumbh. I have failed, Gurudev."

"No, you didn't fail. You bought him back. I saw both of you traveling." Tej heard a soft voice. He thought it was Manika's voice, but saw another girl walking towards them.

"She is Saavi, another of my disciples, who is honing her time-reading skills under me." Rigu gave a short introduction. "What did you see, Saavi? Tell us."

"It was genius of you, Tej. You took a calculated risk, and it worked." Saavi smiled.

"It worked?"

"Yes, it did. I saw both of you traveling back from 2024 AD. When you touched your forehead to Kumbh's forehead, his anchor to this time-slice was reestablished. And when you traveled back, you dragged him along.

Kumbh is again inside this body." Saavi pointed to Kumbh's vessel, lying on his side, still tied in chains. Tej took a sigh of relief.

Rigu beamed and patted Tej's shoulders. "Amazing, my boy, you did it. I will be honest with you, I had my doubts. But you did it."

"Where is Manika, Gurudev?" Tej had a weird feeling that something bad happened to Manika.

"She had to go somewhere, Tej. But we don't have time for these questions. We have to move fast." Rigu signaled Gajendra to get into action. "Gajendra, first administer the de-tranquilizer on Kumbh's body. We need to awaken Kumbh before we give him a dose of the toxin which we prepared from Tej's blood."

"Toxin, Gurudev?"

"Yes, it the neurotoxin in your body, using which you entrapped Vetri in his body twenty years ago. We will do the same to Kumbh. While you were gone, we took a sample of your blood and sent it to our lab. Some brilliant chemists at the ashram have extracted the venom out of your blood."

Gajendra picked up a small earthen pot of de-tranquilizing liquid kept on a table nearby. He dripped a few small drops of it into Kumbh's mouth. Kumbh started gaining consciousness.

"Good, he is waking up. Gajendra, now give him the neurotoxin. But do so with care. Too much of this toxin may kill the vessel and free up Kumbh's consciousness," Rigu cautioned.

Gajendra wore gloves made of sleek-leather and picked-up another earthen pot. He dropped two drops of the neurotoxin into Kumbh's mouth. But the dose had no clear palliating effect on Kumbh. He was getting more and more agitated by the passing moment.

"It's not working," Rigu said in a grim tone. "Kumbh will escape as soon as he is conscious. We have lost everything." He clenched his hair in anger. Gajendra and Saavi looked at each other. They didn't know what to do.

Tej, already tired from the whole ordeal, felt helpless. His mind was blank. In addition, he didn't completely feel as though he was back in his own body. He was moving his jaw, clasping his fingers into a punch and releasing them over and over.

Rigu saw Tej doing his jaw movements and an idea struck him like lightning. "Bite him, Tej."

"What Gurudev?"

"Bite Kumbh right now. Bite him on his wrist, the same place you had bitten Vetri."

"But Gurudev, we gave him the toxin. It didn't work."

"Forget that toxin. It was in an extracted form of the chemical. Your original neurotoxin, running in your bloodstream, may have a different effect. Do it, just do it!"

"But bite him?" Rigu's strange demand perplexed Tej.

Rigu fumed with anger. He clasped Tej's shoulders and roared. "This demon outraged your mother's modesty, tortured both of you for years. Don't you feel that anger, that desire for vengeance? Bite him right now, for your mother, for yourself. Trap him in this body forever. Do it, you son of a bitch!" Rigu fumed with rage as his face turned red and his body palpitated with anger. A few drops of saliva dripped down his trembling chin. Tej, Saavi, and Gajendra were shocked to see their Guru reacting in such a fit of rage, and even using swear words.

Kumbh's body jolted, and he opened his eyes with a loud scream. Tej immediately jumped onto Kumbh while he was still tied and jabbed his teeth into Kumbh's wrist. Kumbh writhed in pain and let out a great cry. Even though he was tied in chains, he was struggling violently. With a strong push, Kumbh broke the chains and pushed Tej with his full strength. Tej flew several feet across the room and crashed into a wall. Saavi rushed outside to get more help. Gajendra sprinted towards a corner and grabbed a thick iron rod.

Kumbh was now fully active. He got off the cement block and eyed everyone present in the room. Even Tej's venomous bite had left no impact on him. He tilted his head sideways as if to stretch his neck and flexed his old muscles.

He looked at Rigu and pointed his finger at him. "This fool may have brought me back, but don't think for a moment that you have won. I am leaving this body and going away. You took your best shot at me and failed. But heed my words—this time I am coming for you. And when I come for you, you won't even know what hit you."

"Oh, you are not going anywhere, Kumbh." Rigu smiled. "You can't see it, but there is a small, faint blue line around your neck, decorating it like a necklace of shackles. Tej's neurotoxin has worked again, just as it worked on Vetri twenty years ago."

Kumbh touched his neck, trying to feel the ring, but couldn't.

"You can see the same ring on your brother's neck, which is an indication he is trapped in his vessel forever." Rigu comfortably sat on a chair nearby. His ultimate aim had been accomplished. Kumbh was trapped.

Kumbh ran to his brother's body. Rigu was right; those marks were there. There was a faint blue line running across Vetri's neck.

Kumbh fumbled across the room, looking for a mirror, but couldn't find one. He immediately tried to leave his own body. There was a slight pink gaze in his eyes, and light pink fumes came out of his mouth but got sucked in again. He struggled to leave again and again but failed. He gaped at Rigu in anger.

"All this is because of you. I will destroy this vessel of yours." Kumbh charged towards Rigu but felt a sharp blow to his skull. Gajendra had hit him with the iron rod. Kumbh fell to his knees and dropped unconscious on the ground.

"Gajendra, put this demon back onto the cement block, and this time, get stronger chains to tie him," Rigu ordered. Gajendra didn't move from his place. He was too dazed.

Tej got up and walked to the center of the room, where Kumbh was lying unconscious. He turned towards Guru Rigu, bowed his head, and clasped his hands together in respect.

"Thanks, Gurudev. Because of you, I have been able to avenge my mother. I have accomplished the greatest goal of my life."

Rigu smiled. "This demon had planned to kill billions of people in future. You have saved countless lives today, son."

Tej dropped to his knees before Rigu and touched his forehead to Rigu's feet. Rigu blessed him. Then, at once, Rigu cringed in agony and got up from the chair.

Tej had bitten the upper part of Rigu's foot, digging his teeth deep into his flesh, into the great saphenous vein.

"What did you do, you fool?" Rigu was shocked and

fumed with anger. Gajendra ran towards Tej and punched him hard on the face. Saavi, who'd just returned with a few disciples and witnessed the scene, was appalled too. *Why would Tej bite his own Guru?*

Tej's first bicuspid tooth had dislodged from the strike of Gajendra's meaty punch. His jaw bled, but he did not complain. Instead, he had a faint smirk on his face. He looked in Rigu's eyes and moved his index finger across his own neck. He was signaling for Rigu to inspect his own neck.

Rigu ran to the corner of the room, opened a box, and took out a small mirror. He examined his neck. There was a similar blue line now visible.

Rigu was a time-demon.

"What happened, Guru Rigu? Or should I say—Rigasur?"

Rigu turned back and promenaded toward Tej. He had a furious smile on his face. "Well played, Tej. I knew Kumbh would tell you the truth about me, but I was sure you wouldn't believe him. You respected me a lot for saving your mother's life and your own. So I took a chance on you. But I underestimated your intellect. You are very smart. You are a time-demon after all."

Tej braced himself as Rigu walked towards him. "No, Rigasur, my primitive brain could not have connected the dots. But being inside Ravi's brain helped me see the events as they were. Ravi's neural constructs will stay with me forever. They help me think better."

Rigu frowned. He had underestimated Tej's ability to learn from his vessel's brain—a brain with the intellect of a delinquent mastermind who ran an international crime syndicate.

"I was looking for my enemy in the abandoned castles

of distant future, yet my foe was right by my side all along. But you must be thinking of how I sensed the evil in you, 'Gurudev'?" Tej lampooned.

"I'm not thinking anything, you fool. My vessel is that of a frail old sage. Your toxin will knock me out in a couple of minutes." Rigu sat on the chair and jammed his palms on his forehead, as if in deep pain.

"Tej, I too saw Kumbh talking to you when he called Guru Rigu a time-demon," Saavi spoke. "But I thought Kumbh was lying, weaving a false story. How did you suspect Guru Rigu to be a time-demon?" She was stupefied. Their Guru, who'd guided them on how to develop their powers of time-reading, was a charlatan? The one who taught them why time-demons were monsters was one himself?

"Several details, when looked at together, pointed to him," Tej replied. "Rigu coming to me after twenty years. Him choosing to reveal that I, too, am a time-demon, and also that I am Kumbh's son. And then, motivating me to be a hero in some kind of battle to save humanity. It felt strange.

"Also, when Kumbh told me that Rigu was, in fact, Rigasur, I was not surprised. Why? Because somewhere inside me, I knew that Rigu's intentions were not as pure as he portrayed them to be. My thoughts were blindsided because he saved me and my mother twenty years ago, but the tower of doubt grew with every new piece of information."

Tej paused. Saavi and Gajendra stood there, wearing perplexed expressions.

"The series of signs did not end there. When I returned to this time-slice, Manika was not here. Why? I gathered that Rigu has either captured or worse, killed her."

"Oh, how did you suspect that, brilliant chap?" Rigu looked up. His eyes were dull and drowsy.

"It was easy. Manika would have seen the events of day seven in her updated time vision. In that vision, she would have seen Kumbh exposing your true face. Curious about you, she would have focused her time-reading on your past. She would have realized that you, in fact, are a time-demon in the guise of a time-reader."

"Smart!" Rigu mocked.

"You knew that she would witness this conversation. You most probably eliminated her right after she saw the time visions of day seven. Her time readings were complete, and she had fulfilled her purpose for you."

"Astute deduction, my boy." Rigu clapped sardonically. "Although I did not kill her. I only captured her. Such powerful time-readers are tough to find and cultivate. I intended to keep blackmailing her for time-readings by threatening to kill her family. Anyhow, go on with your nifty deductive story. I want to hear more." Rigu had difficulty keeping his eyes open. The neurotoxin released in his blood had not only entrapped him in the body but also had a delirious effect.

"The anger you exhibited a few moments ago, when I hesitated to bite Kumbh, that was the final nail in your coffin. A respected, well-read sage, if genuine, would have rarely used a swear word as you did. Even in the state of extreme pain and anger, sages keep their calm. Patience is their first virtue," Tej completed.

Rigu took several light breaths, attempting to stay conscious. "Huh. I had planned to reveal myself to you sooner than later. We could have ruled the world together—though not in this primitive past, but in the super-advanced distant future. This fool Kumbh had plans to slaughter them all. I had different ideas." Rigu's eyes were half closed because of delirium.

"I am not interested in your plans for world domination, Rigasur. I have only one question for you. Where is Manika? Where have you imprisoned her?"

Rigasur laughed. "Why would I tell you that? Thanks to your snake-bite, I am already trapped in this vessel. I also know that after I pass out, you're going to put me in in some deep dark hole. You will not let me go. What do I have to lose? What's your leverage here? But one thing I can tell you for sure, this is not over yet. I will return from the…" Rigasur collapsed on the ground, unconscious.

Tej expounded the whole story to Saavi and Gajendra. They would not have believed a word had they not witnessed this whole incident themselves. While they were envisaging what to do next Gajendra went out and returned with two heavy iron chains.

Tej suspected that Gajendra was actually Rigasur's accomplice, and knew about his secret identity. Gajendra had been with Rigasur for several years, but Tej decided he had no choice except to trust Gajendra.

He knew if he could find Manika, she could time-read Gajendra's past and find out the truth. With the help of a few other disciples, Tej and Gajendra trammeled both Kumbh and Rigasur with thick iron-chains, then called masonry experts and put them on the task of fortifying the chamber.

After that, Tej and a few other disciples started a manhunt around the ashram for Manika. They opened several meditation rooms which had been closed for ages. They searched in food storage halls and warehouses. But there was nothing—she was not found anywhere.

Then one disciple told them about another small, secret ashram. It was a series of small sheds a few kilometers away from the main ashram. Rigu went there often for solitary worship, and he used to be gone for a few days at a stretch. Only a few select disciples knew this. Being loyal followers, they would not have shared this information with anyone. But the news that Rigu was a time-demon had spread and had shattered their trust.

Secret Ashram | an hour later

Tej, Gajendra, Saavi and forty other disciples rushed to the secret ashram. There was a group of seven huts made of red bricks surrounded by a metal fence on all sides. There was one large metal gate, and five muscular men were guarding it.

At first, those guards acted tough and asked the disciples to get lost. But seeing an angry group of forty in front of them, they toned down. Gajendra, clutching one guard by the neck and lifting him three feet above the ground, also helped. Disciples tied them to trees. They conceded that they were each being paid twenty gold coins per month for the guard duty of this secret ashram. Where a sage such as Rigu found so much money was still a mystery. When Tej and Gajendra started breaking the locks and opening those huts, the conditions inside those rooms were appalling.

Several people were being held prisoners in those huts in inhumane conditions. Most of them were time-readers who at some point in their discipleship, had accidentally read Rigu's past. They had realized that he was a time-demon. When they confronted him or tried to escape, he imprisoned them here. They were tied and tortured. One of them had also died two days ago, and his cadaver was left there to rot.

Tej also found Manika in one shed and was relieved to find her alive. On seeing Tej, she cried. She had been beaten and starved. With her torn clothes, disheveled hair, and a wounded jaw, she looked like a different person. The prisoners were freed and taken back to the ashram using horse-carts. Tej realized the primitiveness of this time-slice. If only they had the ambulances of the year 2024 AD! Vehicles and instruments of the current time appeared so archaic to him. Having seen the technologies of the future, the past looked like the Stone Ages.

20
A HEAVY PRICE

anika took two days to get well enough to speak. One morning, as she sat sipping her herbal tea on her bed, Tej visited her.

"How are you doing, sister?"

"I am good, Tej. I couldn't thank you earlier for saving my life."

"You don't need to. You helped me accomplish an act of revenge for which I waited my whole life. I wanted to see if you are doing better. Also, I still cannot wrap my head around a lot of things that happened in those seven days, so I have a lot of questions."

"Okay?"

"But they can wait until you get better."

"No, go on, Tej. I am bored to death lying here all day long, sipping these bitter medicines. I am not sure if this medicine has healing properties, but its taste definitely has damaging properties."

Both laughed.

"How can a time-reader be bored, sister? You can have any vision you want, at any time. And you can enjoy reveling in those visions. No?"

"I haven't done a time-reading in last few days. It takes too much strain. Besides, there is one vision of future which has been haunting me for a long time." Manika narrated to him the whole vision from 2072, where Kumbh planned to take billions of lives by entering the body of Karlesha Breathnach and using Concordia VX to rain havoc.

"Then by capturing Kumbh, we did save a lot of lives. I am not sure why Rigasur spent so much effort pursuing a good deed, Manika. What did he gain from all this?"

"Though the result of his efforts may appear to be positive, his ultimate aim was not noble at all. While Kumbh wanted to murder those billions, Rigasur wanted to rule them like a ruthless dictator. He would have re-configured Concordia VX to control those brains. Imagine—within a fraction of seconds he would have earned billions of slaves, all of them ready to move on his command.

"He would have created vast armies of soldiers to serve his security. Vast harems of beautiful damsels for his carnal pleasures. Huge factories of workers working to build massive monuments for His Excellence, Rigasur. He would have established his own empire on the whole planet. That's what time-demons are usually after. They want either death, destruction, or absolute power over the world. Kumbh was motivated by the former, while Rigasur was aiming for the latter."

"And he used me as a pawn by fueling my fire for revenge."

"Yes, Tej, that is why he actually came to this time-slice thirty-five years ago. Here, he took an old sage's body as a vessel. He also morphed his name from Rigasur to Rigu. His deception and con were so shadowy that people around him did not suspect him. His usual point of stay is far in future, his favorite years being 2035 to 2060 AD. Those will be the times when robotics and technology will give the best fruits to mankind, after which it will start to become a curse."

"Hmm. And who was that other kid who called himself Tej and who came in with a fancy weapon?" Tej grimaced as he re-imagined the kid being shot down by Kumbh.

"Oh, him? I am not sure, Tej. I did see him in the time vision, and I was surprised, too. I have yet to time-read him."

"Wow. I envy you time-readers. You have the power to know anything you want."

"I wish that were true. We can only time-read a target we want to focus on, and that target is not always clear. Being a time-reader is like having access to a library full of infinite books, but not having any idea of what to read, unless you open one of the books and it leads you to the others. Only when I chose to read Rigu's past did I come to know about his true dark self. Anyhow, you had some questions. Go ahead, shoot."

"Yes, the first one. If you knew Kumbh had taken over Samarth Bhasin's body, why did you not tell me before I went to the year 2024?"

"I didn't know that when you started your future journey. As Rigu explained to you earlier, Kumbh had taken good precautions to cover his tracks. We did not know where exactly he was in that city. Imagine sifting through millions of individuals in that city. It's a tedious activity. But several time-readers were re-reading the time visions while you lived those seven days in the year 2024. So, when that person Kevil showed you the seventeen names, it was a huge relief for us. Our potential targets were narrowed."

"Kevin?"

"Yes, Kevin, not Kevil. When he and his friends finalized the seventeen names, I saw that list in my time vision. Using that list, I and a few others could focus our visions on each of those specific individuals. When we did so, we realized that Kumbh's new host was Samarth."

"Samarth Bhasin!" Tej quipped.

"Yes, that one. We decided to give you that name to direct you to the right path. But the problem was how to reach you in the far future. The only artifact going from this time-slice to that time-slice was that wooden box, which we knew you would come for. So we went back to the temple priest and engraved that name on the box. You received the box, with the engraving, in the future."

Tej was impressed. For an instant, he felt awe for what Rigasur had created here. He had gathered several gifted time-readers of this era and put them in a single place. He'd trained them, motivated them, and cultivated their powers. Together, these special individuals could read anything in the past, present or future.

"Another question, sister. When I met Kumbh, he mentioned some massive black doors. What are they?"

"Not black doors, Tej. Black holes, Supermassive Black holes." Manika chuckled.

"Yes, yes, same. He said these black holes are the doors for time-demons to travel through time. How do I understand these concepts better? I am a total novice here." Tej was a little embarrassed, but he knew that to become a better time-traveler, he needed to understand these theories. Calm, serene village life no longer held an allure to him. He wanted to travel to different worlds, spread across time slices, and learn about them.

"You will have a lot of time to learn this, Tej. In fact, you will pick and choose. Time-demons are one of the sharpest species alive on this planet because they have infinite life-spans, which they can use to keep studying. They study philosophy, technology, strategy, music, arts, and whatnot. For you to learn these disciplines, you need to use a concept called pre-dead brain-feeding."

"Brain-feeding? That sounds zombie-isque."

Manika laughed. "You understand Zombies? One trip to the future and you get all the knowledge of the world."

"Ravi's brain is all imprinted here." Tej pressed his index finger on his forehead.

"Pre-dead brain feeding is exactly the same, like imprinting of information. When a person dies, their consciousness leaves their body. But their brain is active for some time before it completely stops functioning. Their thoughts, their learnings, their whole lives are stored there—a book waiting to be read. You can enter that brain only for a few microseconds. When you do so, you imprint that information onto your consciousness. And then you get out before the brain dies completely. That is the concept of pre-dead brain-feeding. You feed on information from a brain before it dies."

"Oh—so I need to do this feeding on selective people so I can learn specific facts."

"Yes. If you enter the brain of a chess player, you can learn to be a grandmaster. If you enter the brain of a quantum physicist, you can understand quantum physics. If you enter the brain of an astronomer who has studied black holes, then you will understand their functioning, too—although avoid some of the famous people throughout history."

"Why avoid famous people? Wouldn't they be the best?"

"They would be, and that is why the pre-dead brains of these famous people will be jam-packed. Many time-demons are entering and leaving the brains of these people all the time. Every time-demon wants to learn from the best. For example, most time-demons interested in learning theoretical physics will be entering and leaving Albert Einstein's brain. Even if it's for a micro-second, his brain would be like a chaotic train station."

"Wait, you said other time-demons? How many time-demons exist?"

"Thousands. Maybe more. Some of us time-readers have attempted to document them. But some madcap time-demon usually comes and destroys those documents. Time-demons don't want anyone documenting them and their movements. The most comprehensive documentation on time-demons was kept in a safe-box at Alakhnanda University in India, but time-demons destroyed it three times. The last destruction happened in 1193 AD. Another copy exists, but time-readers of the future have kept it buried inside the deep dark web, an electronic copy safe behind thousands of fire-walls and cryptic mazes."

"Why not have several copies, Manika? Why only one?"

"Time-demons can use that information to attack each other, settle their old disputes. Whenever two time-demons are locked in a battle, there is a lot of collateral damage to human lives. Hence, we time-readers keep only that one copy. We can read it whenever we want, using our time visions."

"If I go to the future, how can I find this copy?" Tej

was curious to know more about time-demons.

"Sorry, Tej. As a time-reader protocol, I cannot tell this to a time-demon. I have already told you more than I should have." Manika pressed her lips together. She had time-read Tej's past, and she knew she could trust him. But this protocol had been put in place after great deliberation, and she did not want to break it.

Tej could understand the mistrust she was feeling for time-demons in general. She was deceived and tortured by one for days. He changed the topic.

"So the apocalyptic future, has it changed? The events of the year 2072, will they still happen? Now that Kumbh has been trapped inside his old vessel, the flow of the future should be different. Right?"

"To be honest, Tej, I don't know. At times, very discreet paths to future somehow lead to the same outcome. I have attempted re-reading that vision multiple times in the past few days. But there is a problem."

"What problem?"

"Whenever I attempt to read anything after November 18th, 2072, I only get blank visions. It's as if an unknown force is preventing me from reading it."

"Maybe you are facing this difficulty because you are still recovering and are not yet fit?"

"No. I can still see various other solid-reference time visions. I can view them perfectly."

"Solid what?"

"Solid reference time visions. We time-readers usually have a sense of sure-shot events, events which are definitely untouched by any time-demons. One example is the original Big Bang of our universe, which happened billions of years in the past. The second one is the Big Crunch of the universe which will happen billions of years in the future. These events are colossal astronomical happenings. It's impossible for time-demons to alter them.

"These two visions are intact for me, so my time-reading abilities have not been affected. An unknown power has prevented me from looking beyond that date. It's an alien force and is disparate from anything I have ever experienced. I need to talk to other time-readers to find out if they're also facing this vision blockade."

"All right. I reckon that I need to do a pre-dead brain feeding of seasoned time-readers such as you. Then I will understand these complicated concepts with ease," Tej joked, and Manika smiled.

"Time demons have many powers, Tej. You have only realized one. Do you know you can even be present at more than one location in different time-slices at the same time? You can be in the year 5176 BC and the year 4042 AD at the same time."

"What? How?"

"By traveling through time at a rapid pace you can spend only a micro-second in one host. And then travel to another host in another time-slice. And then back. By being missing for a micro-second from a host, you won't lose the continuity of that time-slice."

"So two places at once? That's very convoluted."

"It only requires practice, Tej. One of the ancient time-demons, Monothiaz, was the master of multi-hosting. She once fought simultaneous wars in seventeen different time-slices!"

"Every time I talk to you, Manika, I get to learn a few new concepts. But some of those concepts are too baffling for me, like this one. Even if I could do this multi-hosting, why would I want to be in two places?"

"If your nemesis time-demon is fighting you in more than one place, you need to be present in all those time-slices to counter him or her."

"I need not learn this then. I don't have any nemesis." Tej smiled.

"You took down Kumbh. You had your revenge. But who freed him from the time-prison in the first place? That could not have happened without the involvement of another time-demon. So Kumbh was not acting alone. And when you choose one side, the other side automatically becomes the adversary."

"Then it's good that we chose the righteous side."

"Did we, though? We sided with Rigasur. Had you not identified his true nature, we would almost have helped him become a merciless despot. And even if we saved billions of lives, our actions are still stained with blood. How many soldiers lost their lives trying to infiltrate that castle and capture Kumbh, and how many died while protecting him? Let's not kid ourselves, Tej. This was a war, and in a war, there is nothing right or wrong, nothing righteous or immoral. It's two sides fighting for victory. That's it."

Tej was speechless. Manika was right. She had been Rigasur's disciple for several years. His dark deception had left indelible marks on her persona and self-confidence.

"I'm sorry for the outburst, Tej. I did not mean to be harsh to you." Manika calmed herself. She realized that Tej was not the right subject for the anger and bitterness she was harboring for Rigu.

"No, it's all right. Whatever you said is a bitter truth we have to endure for the rest of our lives. You should take a rest, Manika. I am irritating you more by bombarding you with my silly questions. Tomorrow morning, I will travel to my village. I'll meet my wife, my daughter, and my foster parents. It's been only a few days, but it seems like ages."

"Your wife and daughter? But you are not married."

"What are you saying, Manika? I am married and I have a daughter. Her name is Kaalpriya. Did I not show you the small bangle which she gave me before I left my village? I misplaced it somewhere in the ashram." Tej looked at Manika with a hope that she would remember. He thought perhaps her memory was shaky because of the past few days of atrocities she had endured. But she nodded her head in negation.

"No, Tej. I am sure you haven't mentioned your daughter and wife to me. In fact, Guru Rigu had me read your whole life before he brought you to the ashram. I read most of the major incidents of your life at that time. You were not married. Village elders arranged for your marriage with a girl. But right on the day of your marriage, your mother left for the heavenly abode. As a result, you broke off the marriage. I remember that vision."

"No, Manika, that's not the case. My mother expired three years ago, not five. And I got married to Damayanti five years ago. Our daughter Kaalpriya is four now. Is it possible that the events of the past few days have jarred your memory?" Tej smiled.

Manika did not flinch. Tej thought that she was messing with him for a moment, but her expression was dead-serious. She looked at him for a couple of seconds, then closed her eyes. Her eyelids were shut but Tej could observe her eyeballs moving.

"Manika, are you all right?"

After a few moments, she opened her eyes. "I went

through a few events from your life, going five years in the past. It's the same as before. Your mother died five years ago, right on the day of your wedding. When that happened you refused to go ahead with the marriage. The girl's name was Damayanti. She later married another man named Vilom. That's the same vision I had earlier. I also read the present—you have no daughter."

"How is that possible? I remember spending time with them. I remember kissing my wife, hugging her. Playing with my daughter. Those are not false memories. Tell me what's happening, Manika. Give me some answers!" Tej was about to cry.

Manika controlled her tears, but her throat was heavy. She realized that Tej's actions had led to a re-balance of events. Attempting to change the future, he'd inadvertently changed the past too.

Time travel to the future caused significant changes to the entropies of the events of the future, causing more disorder. This disorder often reverberated back to the past and caused imbalances in the entropies of the events of the past, thereby altering them too. For power-hungry time-demons, such changes were of no consequence. But Tej felt deceived. A loved one being dead was different. One could make peace with such a tragic event. But a loved one who never existed, it was beyond Tej's comprehension.

Manika did her best to explain this phenomenon to Tej, but he couldn't understand it. He was devastated. His throat was heavy with emotion, and his eyes were wet. He sat thinking through the events of these past few days. His quest for revenge ended with an overwhelming cost to him. He remembered what he said to Rudrakshini. "If there's a price attached to your help, I will gladly pay it. Whatever it is."

Those words echoed inside of him, and he burst into a bitter cry. Manika, too, had tears in her eyes. She knew any words of consolation would be futile. It was too big a loss for Tej. It was as if the universe helped him get his revenge, but it had extracted a heavy price in return.

EPILOGUE

Rigasur's body was kept in the chamber of time travel on a similar cement block, next to the bodies of Kumbh and Vetri. Like them, he was also bound in heavy metal chains. One week had passed since Tej imprisoned him.

It was an hour past midnight, and a light mist had engulfed the ashram. Two guards were stationed outside the chamber where the time-demons were kept.

They were half-asleep when three women attacked them. The assailants wore long, dark robes. Their faces were covered with hollow-eyed demonic masks. They pressed anesthetic-dipped cloths over the noses of the guards and subdued them within a matter of seconds.

After hiding the bodies of those guards in bushes nearby, the attackers opened the lock on chamber's door. They sneaked into the room without making much noise.

One woman walked in the front like a leader, and the other two followed her. They strode to the center of the room, surrounded Rigasur's body, and stood there for a few seconds. Rigasur had been tranquilized and showed no movement at all. His breathing was feeble, his pulse was low as if his body was frozen.

The leader bowed down and whispered in Rigasur's left ear. "I kept my promise, my friend. I came here in person to commend you for getting rid of Kumbh. You executed the hardest part of the plan with finesse. I feel sad that you underestimated the kid and in the process martyred yourself. We will miss you in the refurbished seventies. But don't worry, we'll get what we want—with or without you. Happy sleeping, mate!" The leader smirked and sauntered out of the room, followed by the other two women.

Rigasur lay there unconscious, unaware of the surroundings. For a moment, the index finger of his right hand flickered a little.

THE END

LIKED THIS BOOK?
READ MORE FROM THE AUTHOR

TIME
CRAWLERS

Alien Invasion, Dark Artificial-Intelligence, Time-Travel, High-Tech Hindu Mythology, Djinn Folklore, Telekinetics, and life-consuming cosmic entities are some major themes in this book. Author has woven these themes into six tightly-knit, fast-paced Sci-Fi stories

A brief introduction to the stories:

1. Nark-Astra, The Hell Weapon: The weapons he possesses make him the destroyer of worlds, and he burns for revenge. A high-tech take on ancient Indian mythology.
2. Death by Crowd: The dark desires of the masses; darknet websites fueled by a crypto-currency. What lurks in the background - an advanced artificial intelligence?

3. Genie: He rubbed a lamp alright, but what he got was the shock of his life. A sci-fi take on the djinn myth.
4. Time Crawlers: There are individuals who exist in multiple time periods at once, and there are those who know about them....
5. Eclipse: No attacks, no blood-shed, yet there was an invasion and a conquest. Who are these shapeshifter aliens being hounded by an eclipse?
6. The Cave: The fate of an advanced imperial race hangs in balance as a dark celestial entity meets a legendary protector.

Reader Reviews:

"Time Crawlers is a highly imaginative, gutsy and spellbinding book of 6 stories that take us on a morally challenging ride through high-tech worlds and encounters that shock, terrify and enthrall us."

~ Peter

"Well-written and fun collection of short stories that kept my interest. The author gives us something to think about. How much of our current reality is real and how much is illusion?"

~ Cheryle

"I wasn't sure if I would like this book going in because I usually don't read hardcore science fiction. .. However, this set of short stories was very interesting and kept me reading. I would

recommend it to anybody that likes sci-fi or futuristic stories. "
~ Cailin

"Quick and super-enjoyable! Kind of like a collection of X-files + moral philosophy + AI + dark web + plot twist mash-up super bonanza! One of the stories in particular, Death By Crowd really stood out to me. It dominates that super-creepy-cause-it-could-be-true vibe."
~ Mara

"Time Crawlers is a gripping and fun read. Varun Sayal's writing is incredibly imaginative and original. I enjoyed every second of reading this short compilation of out of this world stories. If you are a fan of science fiction you should definitely pick up this book."
~ Lauren

"This book has definitely sparked my love for Sci-Fi book to the next level. Absolutely amazing concept."
~ Katherine

"Time Crawlers was my favorite. I know... that's the short story that gave the book it's name. But seriously the concept of that

story made me think about life, past, present and future and I just loved that."
~ **Jessica**

"Time and tested subjects of invasion, conquest, AI taking over coupled with Djinns and powerful missile-like weapons from Hindu folklore, make for an engaging and diverse cocktail in this book. Must buy, an engaging read."
~ **Ankita**

"Damn Good! The author takes us through a roller-coaster ride of a breath-taking narrative. Considering how vast the field of science fiction is, he weaves some mean tales."
~ **Shatarupa**